About the Author

Brenda Beckford is the author of *Light Finds Love*, she had JD in law, and she was the recipient of the Deans Award from Massachusetts School of Law. Her love of researching and her love of history come together beautifully in this historical romance book. She has researched this period extensively, learning about the daily life of the people in this region to infuse her characters with depth, context, and realism. She lives in Chicago with her husband, their wonderfully large, blended family, and their beloved dog, 'Bender'.

Light Finds Love

Brenda Beckford

Light Finds Love

Olympia Publishers
London

www.olympiapublishers.com
OLYMPIA PAPERBACK EDITION

Copyright © Brenda Beckford 2024

The right of Brenda Beckford to be identified as author of this work has been asserted in accordance with sections 77 and 78 of the Copyright, Designs and Patents Act 1988.

All Rights Reserved

No reproduction, copy or transmission of this publication may be made without written permission.
No paragraph of this publication may be reproduced, copied or transmitted save with the written permission of the publisher, or in accordance with the provisions of the Copyright Act 1956 (as amended).

Any person who commits any unauthorized act in relation to this publication may be liable to criminal prosecution and civil claims for damage.

A CIP catalogue record for this title is available from the British Library.

ISBN: 978-1-80439-745-9

This is a work of fiction.
Names, characters, places and incidents originate from the writer's imagination. Any resemblance to actual persons, living or dead, is purely coincidental.

First Published in 2024

Olympia Publishers
Tallis House
2 Tallis Street
London
EC4Y 0AB

Printed in Great Britain

Dedication

I dedicate this book to Phanuel Boysie Ramorobi, "Esquire the light of my soul."

Acknowledgements

Thanks to my husband, Umaru Kato; for encouraging me and to my mother Florence for always giving me wings to fly in everything I do including writing this book.

Prologue

Samantha Rachel-Anne Minnis, the only daughter of the Honorable Sir Walter Minnis Esquire and Viscountess Lady Lucile Monroe, sat in a tight ball hidden inside her late father's stuffy oak desk. She was tucked in a secret compartment underneath the desk, where the chair would be pushed in. Even if someone sat in the chair, they'd never detect her presence. She was impatiently awaiting her grandmere and her older brother, Bart, to enter the study so she could eavesdrop. She hated to stoop to anything as unladylike as eavesdropping, but desperate times called for desperate measures. After years of uncertainty, she had at last reached desperation *tonight*.

She'd endured more than her fair share of losses in her young life. She was now nine and ten, and she'd borne all her losses with a stiff upper lip, till now. Mostly because she'd been able to share her grief late at night with her servant and only true friend, Healey O'Malley. In private, the girls dropped their titles; it was just Samantha and Healey (not mistress and servant). At night, Healey would crawl out of her cot in the servant's quarters and tiptoe up to Samantha's rooms in the upstairs chambers. They'd both lay on Samantha's fine feather bed, all smiles and giggles, telling each other fanciful stories in hushed whispers all night.

However, those smiles had turned to tears these past years. Healey would hold Samantha's hand while Samantha cried out her sadness and grief over the death of her parents. And now Healey was leaving too? Bart had informed Samantha at luncheon that afternoon that she would lose Healey tonight too. Healey was her last remaining friend and confidant. Why tonight? Why Healey? Tonight, Samantha meant to find out.

Questions abounded in Samantha's head as she waited silently within her hiding place under the desk. *Why was Healey being sent away? And where, for that matter, had all of Evansdale's heirlooms gone to?* Her once lavish home was starting to look like an abandoned palace.

"Tonight, once and for all, I'm going to find out what is really going on at Evansdale Manor." Samantha resolved hotly under her breath, her remarkable waist-length blonde hair bobbing vigorously as she tucked her adult body securely under the desk.

Luckily, no one had seen Samantha enter the study an hour earlier. Her former childhood governess, Mistress Bertha Walformought, had been a tight-lipped old termagant. Mistress Walformought had constantly locked Samantha in her nursery room (without supper at the slightest of infractions). As a result, Samantha had learned how to sneak out of her locked rooms in the nursery undetected by age four. She'd then found and accessed the servant's stairs, where one night she ran into six-year-old Healey, the cook's daughter.

Healey had just pilfered two ginger cookies from the cooling pan and was hastily stuffing one inside her mouth when she'd bumped into four-year-old Samantha.

Samantha, who had only eaten water and bread for two days, as punishment for not knowing her multiplication tables, stared hungrily at the last ginger cookie, and Healey reluctantly gave it up, shrugging. The two became fast friends and instant confidantes, and with Healey's help, Samantha gained access to the food in the servant's quarters. More importantly, Samantha now had access to the servant's stairs, thus allowing her to come and go as she pleased from her nursery while the governess thought she was in her rooms. Her and Healey had become best friends from then on.

At night, Samantha roamed freely in the inner servant's maze of the mansion, while the old warthog thought she was asleep. Eventually, the old hag had wised up to Samantha's escapades, she'd blocked the servant's entrance, and double-barred the nursery doors as well, effectively locking Samantha in her rooms for days at a time. All the while admonishing Samantha's doting parents from interfering.

"She's my charge, and she's sorely lacking in discipline. You've spoiled her rotten. My methods are unorthodox but effective."

The stalwart matron had huffed, her massive bosom heaving inside crisp bombazine fabric.

The governess was taller than Samantha's father and mother, and she towered over the couple as she made her next declaration.

"If you interfere, I'll simply have to leave."

Samantha's frail mother had been in tears.

"Oh, Walter!" she wailed.

"What are we to do? All her charges have made spectacular matches, and it's rumored that one of her pupils even married an Earl. But she's so cruel to our little girl. I can't bear it, Walter. I simply just can't bear it!" her mother had cried.

Her mother had descended into severe migraines and was not seen or heard from for days. And her father, sick with worry over his beloved wife and daughter, had settled inside a bottle of scotch and didn't come out until his wife was recovered.

Samantha had resolved then and there to handle the matter of the warthog privately and keep her parents out of it. Perhaps they weren't a match for the old lady, but she was.

*

When Samantha could no longer sneak into and out of the nursery under her own steam, she'd coached Healey, her dearest friend, and servant, on how to send in sustenance via the nursery window using a complicated contraption made with ropes and pulleys. Samantha had designed it herself using her late grandfather's engineering books. Using this system, she'd even managed to sneak in toys, books, and sweetmeats with the vigorous help of the cook. When Bart, her only sibling, was home from Eton College, his help was enlisted, and he became part of her crew. With her own strength, her brother, Healey, and the cook, Samantha persevered and thrived. The cook couldn't abide the stiff, overbearing governess, and he also had a sweet spot for the clever, energetic Samantha.

The result of all this subterfuge was that Samantha developed the nimblest mind of any young lady within 100 acres before age seven. When her brother also rebelled against the warthog, in his defiance, he taught his sister to gamble with cards and play chess. He snuck in through the window while she was locked in her rooms one day and taught her, and she quickly became unbeatable in all games, thus earning herself the title of the cleverest child around.

"A most undesirable trait in any young lady," her mother lamented repeatedly as she watched her six-year-old daughter beat her father at whilst and then checkmate him at chess three times in a row.

"You mustn't be too clever, dear," her mother had warned. "Or you won't be able to find a husband. No man likes a woman who is too smart, especially when she doesn't bother to flatter his ego by letting him win or hide her cleverness. You'll become an old maid."

Her mother had predicted overwrought, and no one knew just how right the lady was.

"Quite right," her father had quipped, ever the lady's supporter in every cause, even against his own children. He'd winked at Samantha to take the sting out of his words.

"Your mother is right. You'll never snare a husband if you're too clever."

Samantha's father winked, his hazel eyes twinkling, as he lost another round of whilst to his six-year-old. He then fluffed Bart's thick brown locks, silently acknowledging that Bart had taught his sister well.

Walter Minnis always knew what his children were up to, but he never had the heart to defend them against their mother. As such, he was a de facto co-conspirator in their schemes but a valueless one since he never spoke up for them.

Samantha hadn't agreed with her mother, though she bowed her head compliantly. *Who cared what a smelly husband wanted anyway?* Nonetheless, to please her mama, she began to hide her immense intelligence behind a benign, serene smile, pretending to be as clueless as a babe. However, after her mama was asleep, she would sneak books into her room and read them in the dim candlelight. She adored her fashionable, beautiful mama, and if appearing dumb pleased her mama, then Samantha would pretend with the best of them. She soon developed a habit of hiding her true intelligence from everyone, even after her mama and papa passed. After her parents' passing, Samantha kept up the pretense of being a clueless blonde-haired ninny with everyone except Bart and Healey.

Healey got Samantha through a series of devastating heartbreaks, the death of both Samantha's parents, the stillbirth of Samantha's little sister Charlotte, and the loss of all Samnatha's friends while they one by one got married and moved away from the country. But Samantha waited patiently for her time to come, outwardly looking serene but inwardly crying her fears of becoming an old maid only to Healey every night.

And tonight, Samantha had been told that she likely would not have a come-out season at all and that she would marry quietly in the country. Her grandmama had looked crestfallen to deliver this news, and since the elderly matriarch and her brother Bart were all that Samantha had left, Samantha had hurried to comfort her grandmama.

"It's all right, Grandmama. I didn't want a smelly old season anyway." She'd lied unconvincingly.

"A quiet marriage in the country sounds lovely."

The dignified lady had sniffed gently and patted Samantha's hand.

"It will be well in the end."

She had said, half-heartedly as she had said so often these days, in her quintessential dignified voice. Though whether this sentiment was meant to comfort Samantha or herself, no one knew.

As if the heartache over her season was not enough, Samantha had also noticed big changes in the estate since her parent's death. Priceless heirlooms, one by one, had gone missing. Every time Samantha inquired about them, grandmama told Samantha that the artifacts were being "cleaned or restored" in London.

Then one by one, the staff became considerably reduced, and tonight her longtime childhood friend and personal maid, Healey, had been released and placed in a good position with another family in London. Quite naturally, Samantha was devastated by this news as she and Healey were extremely close.

Samantha's activities and social calendar had also inexplicably declined significantly; until she was invited to just a few intimate dinners hosted by the local gentry. She now wore the same jewels repeatedly, as all her other heirlooms and jewelry "were being cleaned."

To add insult to injury, her yearly London shopping season with Amy, which she looked forward to every season with glee, was inexplicably canceled. Her gowns, though of fine quality, were dated and desperately needed to be updated if she had any hope to attract a suitor, a fact that Bart seemed to have forgotten or had no clue about.

Bart stalwartly avoided all Samantha's questions since their father's death. He was now the head of household; he dictated her activities and allowance. He seemed determined to use his new power to deny her everything, even her pin money. She was surprised; she'd expected differently from him. She pinned him down, blocking his exit from the library with her body demanding to know what was happening, but he avoided all her inquiries.

But why? The answer was in this library, she suspected. But so far, she hadn't gained access inside. It was always locked, and Bart always kept the key on his person. She sought his attention again this morning after luncheon. After finding out about Healey, she demanded to know what was going on.

Bart had been both silent and grim.

In exasperation, she'd exploded. "When are you going back to Eton?" she'd asked in an uncharacteristically loud voice. A lady never raised her voice, but she was at her wit's end. Her brother had left Eton when their father died two years ago, and he was supposed to have returned to school by now to finish reading for the bar. His dream was to follow their family tradition. Their late father had been a solicitor (in their family, the oldest male read for the bar). Bart had confided to Samantha long ago that he was in love with Serina Broughton, the local accountant's daughter. But, he did not feel worthy of taking her as a bride until the fellow esquires had lifted the golden rod to admit him to the bar. Once a full esquire, only then, would he feel worthy of taking Serina as his bride. But that required him to return to Eton to complete his studies.

"When are you returning," she'd persisted?

"Never!" he'd barked, emotion choking him.

"I'm never returning to Eton, to hell with my studies!"

He'd then stormed out, leaving his porridge uneaten.

The food was another thing that had changed at Evansdale Manor. Gone were the laden platters filled to the brim with kippers, ham, rashers of eggs, bacon, and loads of fresh fruit and fresh bread. In the past baked bread, and spun butter were prepared and ready every morning for the mistress of the manor to break her fast. The plethora of food used to fill the breakfast table completely. *So enormous it was!* The weight of the food dishes so heavy that Samantha had often worried that the table couldn't hold it all.

Whereas now, most days, she was only served sweetened porridge and tea every morning, except on Sunday mornings. On Sundays, she would get coddled eggs and bacon with a small heel of fresh bread with no butter, as the buttery had been "broken" for ages. With Healey gone, the staff size was now just five. Samantha's grandmama had ordered the east and north wings of the estate closed. As such, a small staff could never manage the vast property unless the unused wings were closed.

Night after night, Samantha had noticed grandmama and Bart going into closed meetings in their father's old study when they thought she was asleep. She'd crept downstairs and tried to listen at the heavy oak door several times, but the enormous, thick wood wasn't letting out any sounds. Tonight, Samantha decided "enough was enough"; she was going to find out what was going on here once and for all. But she needed to be inside that room. Luckily, she'd remembered her childhood hiding place inside the desk, and she'd secreted the key from Bart's coat while he was distracted. Not prone to fainting, she'd feigned a faint after the afternoon tea, and as he'd carried her to the settee in the library, she'd silently made a grab for the key.

That night, she'd pretended to have a migraine so that she could be excused early from dinner, putting her plan in place she'd snuck inside the desk while no one was around. Luckily, her petite frame still fit inside the desk, though much more snuggly than she'd remembered. She had been raised as a gently bred young lady, and she knew that eavesdropping was unladylike, but she had to know why all these changes were happening at Evansdale. She was not a child, and she was tired of being treated like one. However, the irony of where she sat in a tight ball in a secret corner of her father's desk was not lost upon her; as well as the fact that despite her great age, she had never even been kissed. With no London season, being holed up year-round in the country, with Bart chaperoning her so closely even at local parties, and with wearing clothes that were two years past the latest season, she doubted she would ever be kissed. She'd likely die a spinster.

What was taking so long? Inside the small space, Samantha smiled, remembering how she and Bart would hide here for hours on end from their governess. Now Bart had completely forgotten the familiar hiding spot since coming of age. Bart was a completely changed man since their parents' death; he looked stressed and harassed all the time. Often, his hair was disheveled and standing straight up as if he were constantly running his fingers through it. He spent long hours in their father's study, and he often had several unhappy-looking gentlemen continually coming in and out of the study. At dinner, he was distant and sullen. Samantha felt like she had lost him, along with her father and mother. *But why? Why wouldn't he confide in her?* They had told each other everything at one time, and they'd sworn an oath to always do so.

Samantha stilled her movements. Someone was coming; it was Bart (speak of the devil, and he will appear.) She smiled at her own bleak humor.

She strained to hear what was going on outside the desk. She picked up on the loud thump of the cane and shuffle that marked her grandmama's approach. She heard the clink of glasses as someone poured out brandy. Then she heard the heavy leather chair scrape the ground as it was pulled away from the desk; next, she heard a heavy plunk as someone sat at the desk. Obviously, it was Bart.

"Your drink is there, Grandmere."

Bart's husky voice came from above Samantha's head. He sounded as if he'd had a few more drinks since dinner. That was another thing Samantha had noted, Bart drank more and more these days, and he used to hate strong drink, especially after he'd seen what it did to their late father.

"I don't like strong spirits. You know that, Bartholomew."

she heard their grandmother's low voice, sounding weary and threadbare.

"A strong bracing cup of tea is my drink of choice, though

today I will take a nip of the brandy on second thought. There was silence as she drank. "Today has been especially tiresome on my nerves." She sighed.

"Oh, Bart!" she wailed suddenly. "Who would have ever imagined it would come to this!"

Samantha had to stop herself from coming out of hiding and going to her grandmama's arms (as she hated to hear her in such distress). *What was wrong?*

"Neither I, Grandmere," Bart said with a slight slur.

"But I have tried everything I can think of to save this family. Walter, may God rot his soul, gave away all our birthrights in his blasted secret gambling addiction. Those sod creditors have been nipping at my heels ever since he died. Do they not think I saw them at the funeral licking their blasted jaws preparing for the kill before that bastard was even cold in the grave?"

Samantha accidentally let out a small "squeak," then quickly covered her mouth, tears welling up in her eyes at the pain she heard in her brother's voice. Never had she heard him speak like this about their late father. The shocking thing is that Grandmama seemed to agree, and there was no scolding about his disrespect to the dead.

"I know all that now, Bart," she said vehemently.

"I would dispatch that old rot to the devil again if I could for what he has done to you and your sister's inheritance, but let's focus now and quickly. The creditors are coming to claim this place by the end of the week if we can't pay down the debt as we agreed to do through our solicitor. We need a thousand pounds by this week's end if we are to keep Evansdale Manor."

"Don't you think I know that, Grandmere? I've sold everything of value in Evansdale that isn't nailed down. I haven't paid the staff in a year; those few that stay on do so only out of loyalty. And I've mortgaged or leveraged all our few remaining assets in the Americas to the hilt. But Walter tied my hands when he signed off all of your and Samantha's estates to his cronies to cover his gambling debts. Your side of the family is where all our wealth came from, and that bastard had no right. He even gambled away Samatha's dowry, which the viscount had put in a separate trust to ensure her future." A loud crash followed as a glass hit metal. Samantha imagined what had happened. It sounded like Bart threw his brandy glass into the fire, and it bounced off the metal fire poker.

"Is there no one? Who will come to our aid then?" whispered Grandmama.

"All the charity balls I've thrown over the years, all we've been and done in the ton. Are we to be forsaken to the wolves so easily, all for a thousand pounds?"

She hiccupped as soft cries came from the direction of her chair.

Samantha wrapped her arms around herself, crying silently at the sound of her grandmama's tears. It was worse than she had imagined—much worse. They were destitute and were about to be thrown out of their home on their ears unless they could come up with a thousand pounds by week's end.

"Nathaniel Sweet approached me again about marrying Samantha," said Bart.

"But I put the toad off. I know how opposed you are to him. Most of the offers we had over the years for her hand have simply evaporated. The ton is pulling rank; evidently, some of the mamas have heard of our troubles, and those that want a big dowry have pulled out. And you know, because of Walter, Samantha doesn't have a title. A title is the only thing the ton loves more than wealth."

"Well, I have a title," Grandmama said.

"And the families that don't stand with us in our time of trouble will rue the day, this old cat still has some tricks up her sleeve. I will write to my old connections abroad. Either way, my only granddaughter will not be disgraced further by these creditors and marrying Sweet is out of the question. I know his predilections for young boys, and I will not subject her to that. If worse comes to worst, we will go abroad indefinitely. I can find Samantha a worthy husband in France. Leave me now, Bart. Come kiss me goodnight and leave an old woman to battle her demons in peace. You are a good grandson."

After Bart departed, Grandmere whispered,

"Mon Dieu." *My God.*

"Mon Dieu, help us, Father," she prayed.

"We need a miracle. We are utterly at our toughest hour." She then recited the Lord's Prayer in Latin. Then the old bird cried, deep soul, racking sobs. Unknown to her, Samantha cried silently along with her. Of all the things Samantha could not bear, her grandmama's tears were chief among them.

Later that night, after everyone had gone to bed, Samantha came out of hiding from the desk, with an iron resolve in her heart. She would fix this, and she would do it without marrying Sweet. The thought of him made her skin crawl! Some of her male cousins loved men, she'd always supported them, but loving little boys was an entirely different matter-one she did not support.

Before departing that night, her friend Healy had passed on the card of a gentleman that had been trying to get word to Samantha for months.

"Here, Miss Samantha," Healey had said through tears.

"I don't entirely trust him, but he said he could help."

The childhood friends then hugged each other and cried, saying their goodbyes. Healey wrote down her London details, where she would be living as personal maid to an Earl's daughter. It was a nice position, and Samantha knew her grandmother had arranged it. She always thought of everyone.

Grandmama, in her old age, deserved better than this sorry situation that Samantha's late father had placed them all in. They all deserved better, and now she knew why her brother hadn't gone back to school. likely, his school fees had been gambled away along with everything else.

Samantha was going to find a way to solve this. She thought late into the night and came up with a plan. While everyone was sleeping, she wrote a letter to Grandmama and Bart, making up a story about visiting a sick friend in the city the next day and that she would be back by nightfall. The whole family knew her best friend Amy was expecting her first child, and they knew how nervous Samantha had been since receiving the news. They would assume that she had gone to visit Amy.

She then wrote a note to the gentleman that Healy had told her about, agreeing to meet with him in a crowded tea shop in London at precisely two o'clock. She woke their only footman and ordered him to deliver the letters right away, instructing him to be discreet. She got a few hours of sleep after her missives were delivered, grateful to their only remaining footman for his loyalty (now that she knew that he and the others hadn't been paid wages in over a year, she was even more grateful for their dedication).

She planned the remaining details of her trip to London and left at first light, in their family carriage, grateful that all of the horseflesh hadn't been sold off. She was on her way to London before Grandmama and Bart woke up.

Chapter One

Gordon Allen clutched the note inside his coat. He was wearing all black clothes. His all black garb made it easier for him to blend into the busy London streets. Allen was the agent for Lord Alexander Leitchfield, Duke of Ennsbury, or "Lord Light," as Leitchfield was known in the seedier parts of London. It was a play on words of course-Leitchfield bore no resemblance to light whatsoever. He always wore black clothes, had dark tan coloring, and even his hair was as black as night. It was rumored that his soul was black as well. Leitchfield was extremely buff for a lord of the realm, and he could fight his way out of a brawl in any London club with the best of them (and he'd done so, on more than one occasion).

Lord "Light" also had a penchant for dark sexual games and often bought sex slaves. Gordon Allen was the unfortunate agent commissioned to hire the willing female partners that would partake in his lordship's games.

"Acquisitions," the lord called them. He even had a pleasure house on the outskirts of London where he stored those "acquisitions." Though the store house was now empty due to some unfortunate rumors.

Gordon Allen was paid handsomely for this role, of acquiring said "acquisitions." Allen had been in his lordship's employ for a long time, ever since retiring from his prior full-time occupation as a bow street runner. Gordon Allen found his services to Lord Light to be far more lucrative and far less taxing on his nerves than chasing thieves across London square. It was a cushy job, and Gordon Allen, who had been an unremarkable bow street runner, felt it suited him far better and paid him far more.

The salary Lord Light paid Gordon allowed Allen to live almost like a gentleman. He had finally been able to say goodbye to his nasty rank boarding room and said fare the ewell to his cantankerous landlady in the slums of London. Allen upgraded his living quarters to a two-room flat in London proper. He now had a cook, a new wardrobe, and a chance to wed Madeleine, the fair-skinned, much sought-after main street florist.

Everything was looking up for Allen. Except, as of late, the comfortable job that he'd secured for himself was getting more and more difficult. The willing partners to play Lord Light's sex games were getting fewer and fewer in supply. Lord Light's reputation had grown darker. Even the more seasoned courtesans were turning Gordon Allen down.

It was all because of a scandal that had broken out last year. A certain spurned countess had spread salacious gossip about Lord Light. As a widower, she had agreed to become Light's mistress. But she'd fallen hard for Light, and he'd coldly ditched her after only three months of intimate association, as was his habit.

After the split, he'd agreed to pay the widower's full financial obligations for a year to ease her wounded pride, but she hadn't wanted or needed his money; she'd wanted Lord Light in her bed-hot and throbbing. Needed him, in fact. She'd reveled in ecstasy as his dark, tan fingers, had played across her fair skin, strumming her body like a lute. She'd mewled plaintively on his shoulder like a newly born kitten every time he'd made love to her. After years of laying unmoved under her inept husband, who'd fumbled under her night dress as if embarrassed; at one and thirty, she'd finally experienced release under Light's lean, unyielding body. She now understood what all the "fuss" was about. And she wasn't about to just let Light stroll out of her life; she refused to go back into sexual frustration. She'd done every outrageous act possible to win him back, but nothing had worked. Rake that he was, he'd simply taken his fill of her flesh, then simply moved on, he never looked back. She'd been incensed, then furious, and finally irate; she was determined to make him pay.

In revenge, she'd spread lewd gossip about him. Claiming that Light had beaten her (and with a rod of all things). She'd further claimed the beating had been so severe that she'd fainted. *Poppycock!*

Yes, the lord did sometimes beat his sex slaves, but only those who enjoyed that sort of thing and never any of his mistresses. And certainly, never an unwilling partner. He'd never beat a consort that didn't agree to such a thing; he wasn't an utter barbarian after all. Besides, there were safe words and all those types of things. But since the countess was a lady, and a widower her word had been taken as gospel on the matter, and Light's name had become tainted. The gossip had spread far and wide, fanned by his fearsome reputation. As such, his name was now as soiled as mud.

As such, no one wanted to engage with Light as a consort. Even the more seasoned girls were wary of him, especially because of how brawny the lord appeared. He was over six feet tall with a large frame, a muscular build, and a lean torso of pure muscle. He was also as strong as an ox to boot.

Gordon Allen had to resort to seedier girls, whom his lordship had flatly refused to have anything to do with. He wanted refined ladies, or at least the appearance of good breeding. And they had to be willing to play his lordship's games (all of their own accord). No coercion, no trickery, no lies—those were his terms; willing partners only.

"I am, after all, a gentleman." Light had barked at Gordon Allen as he'd thrown a sassy London girl with brassy red hair at him and fastidiously wiped his hands as if the girl had the clap. "Bring me another one of those, and it will be your head."

Light had barked!

Gordon Allen wasn't sure if Light meant it, but he took no chances as he walked away from the elegant Dukedom mansion with the girl in tow. Once at a safe distance, he muttered, "What gently bred young lady would agree to be the willing sex slave of a maniacal lord?" He huffed under his breath. *She would have to be desperate indeed, he thought* silently.

"Indeed."

Chapter Two

Luckily, as fate would have it, and Gordon Allen believed in fate, his bow street runner friends had alerted him to the dire straits of a certain Miss Samantha Minnis. She was reported to be a rare beauty, a lady in all respects, minus the title. It seemed her father had gambled away her dowry and all the brothers' entailed estates. Apparently, the father had no legal right to do so, but the family had agreed to pay the debts in installments rather than risk the scandal of going to court. However, the gossips, and the rumor mill had done even further damage than the father had. As such, now no respectable family would allow their sons to marry the girl, even with all her striking beauty.

Pity, Gordon Allen thought as he watched the young lady sip her tea delicately. She looked at her timepiece for the third time since arriving at the tea house thirty minutes prior. In all his years of being an agent for his master, he had never seen a more beautiful woman. She was slender but voluptuous, with bold, striking features and soft full lips. Her movements flowed easily and gracefully, and her complexion was golden, in direct contravention to the dictates of the times. Most young ladies avoided the sun; but she looked as if she bathed in it. As such, all the young ladies around her looked pale and washed-out. She stood out among her counterparts like a rose among thorns. But more startling than her beauty, was her silky waist length hair; it bore every variation of blonde known to man-from light buttercream to deep gold. Even though it was tucked securely under her hat, fine wisps of hair escaped their confines to frame around her face delicately. The overall effect was stunning. Gordon Allen smiled despite himself admiring her allure.

She gathered her belongings to leave, and that was his cue to make his presence known. He had learned long ago, when meeting a mark, to watch and wait as long as possible (in case it was a trap). He bowed to the lady as he slowly approached, saying her name very low so as to not to attract any unwanted attention from the matrons.

"Miss Minnis?" he asked

She nodded and sat back down, looking disapprovingly at her watch, a silent censure. He'd seen her arrive early to their meeting, unlike most ladies, she was punctual.

"My apologies, I was detained by a prior engagement," he lied. He gave her a benign smile trying but failing to put her at ease. She eyed him coolly, her back remained ramrod straight.

She did not return his smile; instead, she formally extended her hand, gave him a firm handshake then waved at a chair across from her (indicating he should sit). She'd selected a quiet corner of the tea house; a spot where they could be seen but not heard. It was a wise choice, especially since she had no chaperone, and she was unmarried (judging by the lack of a ring on her finger).

She lifted the heavy China teapot and tilted her head in inquiry. Gordon Allen nodded. Her long, elegant fingers poured him a cup of tea and, with a deep throaty voice that was also musical, she asked him if he'd like sugar and cream with his tea.

He nodded yes to both (as the seductiveness of her voice sent unwanted shivers down his spine). He placed his black bowler hat next to his gloves on the table, his bald head reflecting off the dim chandelier candlelight in the tea house. Outside passersby's hurried here and there in a bustling crowd, but their area by the window was quiet and elegant. The brightly lit tea house was a popular meeting place for the busy London crowd. Twenty elegantly decorated tables filled the one room tea house, most of the patrons were ladies, their ladies' maids and companions taking a respite from the busy season shopping. Two teahouse servants moved busily, carrying steaming kettles filled with water from table to table. The patrons were mostly ladies. A few hen-pecked husbands sat glumly here and there, pretending to listen to their wives while quietly checking their timepieces.

Gordon sat up straight. For such a seasoned man, he suddenly felt tongue-tied presenting his seedy offer to this refined creature. He was ready to put this whole unpleasant business behind him. In his discomfort, he found himself glossing over the details of the **tete-a tete**, as he explained the arrangement. He made it seem more like a mistresses-protector relationship than what it really was (a sex slave and master arrangement).

Nonetheless, Samantha blushed delicately while he talked. When he'd finished, she said, "For my own reasons, Mr…?"

"Just call me, Stanley." Gordan politely interrupted her not wanting to use his real name. Samantha saw his hesitation and deduced that Stanley wasn't his real name.

"OK, Mr. Stanley," she said dryly.

"For my own reasons, I find myself intrigued by your outrageous offer. But I must ask, why does your employer find it necessary to have an agent arrange these affairs for him? Most gentlemen prefer to arrange their own paramours. Is he deformed in some way, aged, or disfigured?"

Gordon Allen thought for a while about how to respond. It was a very astute question, and it showed that the lady was very intelligent for all of her tender years and obvious inexperience.

She had blushed at the mild descriptions he'd used to explain her duties.

He considered how to answer her question. Despite her family's financial problems, they were very protective of the young lady. It had taken Gordon four months of diligent effort to be able to meet with her. None of her staff would take a bribe or let down their guard around her in any way. He wondered what inspired such devotion in them since he knew most of them had not been paid their wages in at least a year. Many dedicated employees had turned on their masters for much less. But her staff and family had remained devoted to her. He'd waited so long to get this meeting, and with his own coffers dwindling, he didn't want to scare her off. Besides, if he was to have any chance to marry the delectable fair Madeline, he needed a very nice ring. The commission from this transaction alone would solve all his personal financial worries and allow him to get Madeline a very nice ring to boot. Madeline had her pick of swains, the butcher's son, the tax collector's son, and even a banker's apprentice—they all wanted her. But since he had a good post with Lord Light, Madeline strongly favored his suit. Now all he needed was a ring, he'd promised her it would be real gold with a small diamond (no leather ring for his Madeline).

With his own coffers hanging in the balance and Madeline's ring on his mind, he hedged, mentally deciding how much to reveal and what to keep hidden. Ultimately, he kept most of the details hidden.

"My Lord is rather busy, and he is a bit of a hermit." declared Allen, (This much was true).

"He keeps to himself so much so that he is out of touch with the where's and why's of female companionship. As such he finds this type of arrangement much easier." (Another truthful statement).

Samantha nodded slowly, as if what Allen said made sense even though it didn't. Her analytical mind had found and processed all the holes in his story. But for her own reasons, she kept these observations to herself, maintaining her mask of a serene, not too smart female.

Gordon noticed that they were getting a few stares in her direction, as some of the male patrons likely wondered how such an average looking man had managed to snare the attention of a true beauty.

It was time to end the meeting.

Chapter Three

"Miss Minnis, I don't wish to damage your reputation," Gordon said, staring at the other tea house patrons meaningfully. The matron busybodies seemed to also take notice of the fact that Samantha had no ring on her finger and no female escort or chaperone, a few fans starting to quiver as the ladies talked behind their fans.

"I think we should end our meeting shortly," he declared, putting on his hat. "This is what we're offering." He shoved a piece of parchment in her direction, it stated the terms of the agreement.

The contract duration was for six months, all her expenses would be paid, including gowns, cobbler services, hats from the milliners, and new dresses from the seamstresses. She was to limit all her social interaction for the entire duration of the contract and be at the exclusive beck and call of the master. She was to make her whole self available for Light's use in whatever way he saw fit. She would receive 5,000 pounds at the end of the six-month contract. It was all very detailed.

Samantha took out her fountain pen and a small inkpot from her portmanteau and crossed out the 5,000 pounds. In its place, she wrote in 10,000 pounds, paid upfront, and then she signed the document with a flourish and shoved the documents back at Gordon Allen without blinking.

His face turned red, then purple, then white. "Impossible," he whispered, grabbing the parchment. He rolled it up huffily and made to leave.

Samantha calmly sipped her tea and stared outside at the passersby through the window. She looked as if she didn't have a care in the world. If there was one thing she knew from gambling with her brother all these years, it was how to call a buff. She also knew when someone wasn't being honest, and there was something Gordon Allen wasn't telling her. She sensed it.

"Good day, Miss," he said standing, lifting an eyebrow as if expecting her to stop him.

"Good day," she said nonchalantly and coolly went back to sipping her tea.

Gordon Allen stomped off, secretly impressed with the beauty. *If he were only twenty years younger!* That thought stopped him in his tracks. *Who was he kidding? Even if he were twenty years younger! She'd still be out of his league.*

He only got as far as the door to the tea house, when he realized that she wasn't going to call him back. In defeat, he decided to give in. Hell—where else was he going to find another gently bred young lady willing to even give an ear to his outrageous proposal? He was lucky she hadn't thrown her tea in his face, and if she had, she would have been within her rights to do so.

*

Samantha clutched her parasol and her small portmanteau with her clothes in it. In just forty-eight hours, her life had spun in a completely different direction. She had made up a story to her grandmama. "That she would be staying with Amy for a few months" to help Amy with her upcoming baby, as such, she'd be gone for several months, she'd explained. Her grandmama's response had seemed withdrawn and distant.

"Yes, dear, perhaps a break from Evansdale is best for you. Wish Amy my best on the new child. All will be well in the end. I love you."

That was all she'd said.

Samantha had left the 9,000 pounds where Bart would find it; in his study with a note. In the note, she had asked for his secrecy and told him she knew everything. She asked him to pay the money to the creditors. It should buy them time until she could come up with a way to help them save Evansdale.

She used a small fraction of the money to buy a few needed gowns and undergarments. She didn't know much about this Lord Light or where they were likely to go on outings and such, but she knew that a lady should always be prepared for any occasion, even if she was only a mistress (as Gordon Allen had described). She went to see Sophie DeLaRouse. Sophie was the best seamstress in London and the only one her late mother had patronized. Samantha requested that Sophie quickly prepare a few new traveling gowns, day gowns, evening dresses, and a riding habit for her. Luckily, a lady of a similar size and coloring was late picking up her order, the order was immediately transferred to Samantha. All that was needed was a few quick alterations. Samantha's waist was much smaller than the previous clients, so the waist was taken in and the hem let out as Samantha was taller as well. Sophie, having been fond of Samantha's late mother, so she was happy to assist; she even worked late into the night and had the gowns ready the next morning. Sophie adored dressing someone of Samantha's voluptuous shape, trim waist, and golden coloring. Samantha was the perfect canvas to show off Sophie's amazing skill with a needle. As such Sophie even added some inspired French flair to the prior customers' drab designs to bring out Samantha's coloring and amazing shape. All in all, the gowns were amazing.

A visit to the milliner's shop, some lace, leather kid gloves, and new boots from the cobblers, and Samantha felt sure she would be presentable for whatever occasion she found herself in. Pity, she still had very few jewels, but the ones she did have, were stunning and of high quality. They had been gifts from her late mother, and Bart, in his kindness, hadn't allowed them to be sold to their creditors. The thought of the creditors brought a troubled frown to Samantha's serene features. How had her father allowed things to come to this grave impasse. As she rode in the back of the Hackney carriage on her way to her temporary home, she remembered her father. Contrary to most solicitors of the day who were dour and sour-faced, her late father had been handsome in a tall, gangly way. His boyish good looks and pale blonde hair had almost looked silver. Even at nine and thirty, he'd still looked young and dashing. He was always dressed in the height of fashion, even when at home. He'd looked so much like a peer, that even the upper classes often forgot that he was a member of the working class.

On one occasion, Minnis had been walking and talking with Lord Dausghton, the Earl of Gloucester. The pair had been deeply engrossed in a political discussion. They'd stopped at the entrance to Whites, an exclusive gentlemen's club on St. James Street.

Lord Dausghton had signaled for Minnis to precede him at the entrance of the club, which of course, couldn't happen as Whites is an establishment for titled lords only. A red-faced butler had stepped in front of Minnis and denied him entry. The butler had simultaneously stepped aside to allow Lord Dausghton to enter.

"I'd almost forgotten you aren't a member here."

Lord Dausghton had joked, entering and saying his goodbyes to Minnis.

"I sometimes forget you aren't one of us," he'd said casually as he entered his club.

For all his gentile good looks, Minnis was a strong solicitor. He moved so well within the inner circles of the upper classes, that both his prominence and his reputation grew. But like the ill-fated Icarus that flew too close to the sun, many peers felt that Minnis' ambition took him too high; especially when he tried and succeeded in marrying Lady Lucile Monroe, the Viscount's only daughter. Not only was she the season's finest flower, but she was a lady that many of the finest lords had tried to wed and failed. She'd received and turned down not one, not two, but five offers of marriage from the peerage—men not accustomed to hearing a "no" from a female. It stung their collective egos when she said yes to Minnis (a man who was both their social and financial inferior)! To ease their wounded pride on the day of the couple's nuptials, the lords enmasse withdrew their legal work from Minnis' firm. This led to heavy losses for Minnis (losses totaling several thousands of pounds). The lords, feeling confident that they'd sent their message, toasted one another at Whites for a solid week, easing their wounded pride. Thus, ensuring that though Minnis might have the girl they all wanted, but at least he did not also get their money to boot "just desserts for overstepping" Lord Dausghton had declared over his sixth glass of port.

With his finances now tight since the coup from his richest clients, Minnis could no longer afford to live in London. So, he and his new wife retired to the country permanently. He opened a small solicitors office in the town square. Finances were tight early on in the marriage. But because of his lady's popularity, the Minnis family never lacked for entertainment. Even in the country, Lady Minnis threw lavish house parties, soirees, and poetry readings, and her events were always a crush.

Minnis doted on his beautiful wife, she was an accomplished hostess, and she could do no wrong in Walter's smitten eyes; she was his world. To a lesser degree, he also doted on their golden-haired daughter, who resembled her mother to a tee. And to a much lesser degree, also on his only son, the heir, who, being the only dark-haired person in the small family, resembled no one, except maybe Walter the late grandfather.

Chapter Four

It was almost nightfall when Samantha arrived at Lord Light's Mayfield Townhouse, which was located on a quiet, isolated no-through road on the outskirts of London. It looked like any ordinary townhouse on Mayfield Street, except it was very large and sat on a secluded cul-de-sac. The house was plain, it was painted a dull un-assuming white, and it was surrounded by tall green hedges around its perimeter. In short, it was eminently respectable and unassuming.

She paid and dismissed the hackney driver that had brought her to the house with all her belongings. Samantha knocked on the big double doors of Lord Light's home. His aged butler let her in without questions.

"We've been expecting you, Miss," he said.

"You may go straight up the stairs; your bed chamber is to the right on the second floor. There is a maid in there that will unpack your bags and get you anything you need. My name is Bigsby, and I am the butler."

"My," said Samantha, smiling brightly at the dignified solemn gentleman before her.

"That's quite a welcome! Bigsby, I am Miss Samantha M…" She started to give her surname and then thought better of it, biting her lip instead.

The old butler smiled wisely in understanding. She turned her attention to the massive home before her. Her jaw almost dropped open as she took in her impressive surroundings, only long years of practice and training to be a lady kept her jaw firmly in place. Whereas the outside of the house was dull and unassuming the inside, was luxurious and well appointed. Large oil paintings graced every wall, exquisite tall porcelain statues peaked out from every corner, gilded rich crown moldings lined every surface, fine draperies flowed down from tall, massive windows. Expensive mahogany wood furnishings perched archly upon the thick, hand-woven Aubusson carpets. A silver tea set shone brightly in a tall etagere behind a massive, hand-carved Chippendale dining table. She'd never seen a more beautiful sight than all the wealth before her arranged in lavish display.

"It is a pleasure to meet you, Miss Samantha." The butler bowed low over her hand after she'd had a chance to take in her surroundings fully.

"His Lordship sent word that he will be dining with you tomorrow evening, and he would like you to be ready at precisely seven p.m. sharp to join him in the main dining room for dinner."

Samantha simply nodded at a loss for words as she continued to study the stunning rooms about her. She spotted a sleek spinet in an adjoining alcove beside the morning room, her fingers itched to play it.

As Bigsby shut and locked the front door, it clicked with a telling finality. The lock clicked in place; as she heard it, she knew she'd sealed her fate. There was no going back now. Head held high, she climbed the stairs one at a time and found her room. She entered and greeted the maid, breathing a small sigh of relief that at least she would have one night of respite before she met her protector. As Carole (the new maid) greeted her and put her clothes away, Samantha paced nervously before the small fire. The prospect of meeting Lord Light unnerved her. How she wished her mother was still alive. Everything in her life seemed so bleak these days. As she dressed for dinner, she reflected on her beloved mother.

Lady Lucile Monroe-Minnis, the youngest daughter of Viscount Monroe, had been full of light and love. She'd loved to laugh. And she'd been a renowned hostess. Lucille's mere presence brought delightfulness wherever she went, especially at Evandale's Manor. She'd always been surrounded by a bevy of admirers, even after being happily married to Minnis. Her cheerful essence drew admirers out from the fanciest London drawing rooms down to the rural countryside year-round. Her beauty and manner were legendary. The ton's lords weren't the only ones doting on the mistress of Evansdale Manor. The staff adored their beautiful mistress with a fanatical loyalty that hadn't abated even after her death. They simply transferred that loyalty to Miss Samantha. It was a level of dedication that few nobles ever garnered from their household servants.

However, mother and daughter were more different than alike. Lady Lucille had transferred a measure of her mysterious essence to her only daughter but none of her outgoing personality. Samantha was a more somber, intelligent, aloof version of her late mother. On the outside, she was a copy of her mother's face and form; but on the inside, she was an intellectual like her late father, a solicitor, and her late grandfather, an engineer, inventor, and barrister. Samantha had both beauty and brains. A most disastrous mix, according to the ladies of the ton; beauty and brains never mixed well they declared. As a result, Samantha never revealed her true intelligence and inquisitive nature to anyone except her most trusted friends.

Her mother had married below her station when she had married Sir Walter Minnis Esquire, a prominent London solicitor. But all agreed that the couple had made a grand love match. None had seen two people more in love. Nonetheless, the ton, being fickle and prone to putting titles and wealth above all else, did not approve of the match, despite the very real love evident between the two. They felt that it was scandalous for the queen of the ton, as Lady Lucille was called, to choose a lowly solicitor as a husband. A man with no title and no fortune? *Preposterous!* It didn't matter that said husband had steady, respectable employment as a prominent solicitor. Working class income didn't count in their circles. The lords of the ton couldn't stomach the fact that the lady in question hadn't chosen any of them. In retaliation, they collectively set out to make Minnis' life a living hell.

The couple had eloped to the village of Gretna Green to say their vows in Scotland. A year and a half after their elopement, a bonny heir was born to the Minnis family, her brother Bart. The Viscount, who had cut off his daughter initially when she married Minnis, relented after the child was born. He'd watched Minnis drag his only daughter off to the country and struggle to provide for her decently. Her reduced circumstances broke his heart. The Viscount swallowed his pride and gave his only daughter and her husband her full dowry, which included ships as well as lands in the Americas. He also bequeathed the husband full title to Evansdale Manor and transferred his holding and investments from his farmer tenants—income that generated 10,000 pounds per annum to Minnis; to ensure that his only daughter would have a measure of the wealth and luxury to which she was accustomed. But Walter Minnis, for all his scholarly legal intellect, hadn't been raised with wealth. The sheer volume made him giddy, and he became reckless.

The family continued to grow. Next, Samantha was born, and Minnis was now rich; he sold his practice and lived full time as a gentleman (which meant he did nothing). The fickle ton embraced the young couple as if the scandal had never been, even treating Minnis as if he was one of their own (almost, but he was still barred from White's). These had been the happiest days in Samantha's life, she was adored by everyone—by her beautiful mother, by her handsome father, by her maternal grandfather, by her big brother, by the lords and ladies of the ton, and by the entire staff at Evansdale, especially Healey. Life was good except for the warthog (their governess).

However, Samantha's happiness was shattered when her mother died giving birth to her little sister, Charlotte Minnis. After the baby's birth, the poor lady began hemorrhaging. The doctors applied eels to her lower body to heal her, but nothing worked. The sacrifice of birthing the small, red-faced baby had been for naught. The baby passed away two hours after being born, followed by its mother the next day. After both their deaths, Samantha's once happy and cheerful father became a cold, distant shell of a man. He literally drank himself to death, every night he'd crawl into a brandy bottle until one freezing cold morning he was found dead in his shirt sleeves laying on top of his wife's grave an empty bottle of brandy clutched in his lifeless grip. After her parents' death, the ton disappeared into the ethers as if they'd never been only a handful making it to the funeral, clucking their tongues about the tragedy of marrying below one's station (as if that had been the cause of Lady Lucille's death and not the hemorrhaging).

All these tragedies resulted in Samantha never getting her come out season. Viscount Monroe Samantha's maternal grandfather died from grief before Samantha's turned one and five. The same year that Samantha's come-out ball had been planned. Because she was in mourning, over her grandfather's death, her come out ball in London was canceled that year. All her friends of a similar age had their London season, and got married, and subsequently moved away. Samantha was genuinely happy for each of her three best friends as all of them made a slash in their first season and got married. They all married well, many becoming titled, respected ladies running large households of their own. One by one, her other friends also moved out of the countryside of Buckinghamshire to live in prominent homes in London with their husbands; she alone remained behind, unmarried. They'd all made such clever matches for themselves; all the match-making mamas said so.

Even Amy, the least attractive and last to leave from the friend group (even she) was now married and to a Marquis. Amy was now even expecting their first child to be borne by the winter solstice. Rachel, the chubbiest of the four friends, she was now married to a baron. Cecile, the plainest, had also done well. Cecile had been the only one of the four friends that hadn't scored a title in the marriage mart. Cecile married a rich merchant and was now very wealthy. Her husband had not minded marrying a plain girl as long as she had a title. He'd traded his wealth for a title as so many in the working class did. Rumor had it that he had as much money as any titled lord; Cecile lived as comfortably or better than most gentry. Cecile, however, lamented her loss of status; as a merchant's wife, she wouldn't be invited to most of the ton's events. She'd brightened considerably, however, when Amy, a future Marquess, had promised to always include Cecile and her husband whenever she hosted soirees in London. Amy could afford to be generous. Because of her spectacular marriage match, Amy would now have great social pull and would not lose much standing for inviting a merchant's wife to a few events. As such, she chose to be generous, besides, they all loved Cecile, she was unfailingly kind. She accepted her plainness with a grace few women had and instead focused on developing a beautiful spirit.

The girls had turned to Samantha as one, joined in sisterhood commiseration over her plight, of still being unmarried at one and nine. It wasn't lost on any of the newlywed girls that Samantha's beauty far eclipsed each of their own and that if Samantha had gone to London with them, she would have been the toast of the town and married' she likely now would be their social superior. But fate, in its cruelty, had worked against Samantha. For four years in a row, her season had been postponed as such she had remained in the country and never had her official come out. And at one and nine, she was now dangerously close to spinsterhood. Samantha in a rare moment of self-pity had let them embrace her. For once, she lowered her stiff upper lip and let her tears flow freely, the four girls surrounded her with their embrace. She'd hugged each of them dearly, taking in the sorely needed comfort. She no longer believed that all would be well in the end, for her this was the end.

*

Lord Light was fit to be tied. Nothing, absolutely nothing, was going right!

At luncheon yesterday, he had been informed by his secretary that a new sexual acquisition had been delivered for him at his Mayfield residence at the exorbitant price of 10,000 pounds upfront payment, it was double the price of what he usually paid. The money had already changed hands. He had turned red and felt as if he would suffer an apoplexy. 10,000 Pounds? Upfront? *What was she going to do for him? Do somersaults in the air while juggling fruit on her breasts?*

"For 10,000 pounds, she damn well better," he'd murmured to himself. How a mere slip of a girl had outmaneuvered his usually savvy agent? he had yet to discover.

He ordered his carriage to be brought around the next morning at nine a.m. sharp with his bags packed. He would stay the week with her in the Mayfield townhouse. He wanted to meet this oddity at the first opportunity that same day. But again, nothing was going right. His seat at parliament demanded his attention in the assembly that same afternoon, and he couldn't sneak away.

The rest of the afternoon, while in parliament, his thoughts drifted again and again to his newest acquisition. He regretted that he couldn't travel to meet her until the next day. He sent word to his butler to get the young lady settled in and insisted she be ready to present herself to him at dinner the following night at seven p.m. sharp. At that dinner meeting, then and only then, would he take her measure.

What would she be like? Truthfully, every one of his current mistresses bored him to distraction at the moment. It was always the same with a woman; he would be very excited at the beginning of a new relationship and spend all his time with her, only to be bored silly by her in less than three months' time, not wanting to see her again. That's why he'd stopped handling these things himself, hired an agent and made a contract. He wanted to keep it professional, and truth to tell, he couldn't stand the tears and pleading at the end of an arrangement. It wore him down. The breakup with Patricia Countess of Winslow had put him off female hysterics indefinitely. Now he initiated six-month contracts and released the women early if they were no longer to his taste, as was so often the case. *But 10,000 pounds? Bugger! This was intriguing.*

Chapter Five

The following day, at morning's first light, Lord Light set off on the trip to meet the young girl. He had to admit to himself that he was eager. Of course, he wouldn't sleep with her on the first night, as he never liked to rush these things. He had to get to know her first, her likes, dislikes, peculiarities, and whether she had any naughty inclinations.

However, a trip that should have only lasted two hours taken thrice as long because one of his mares caught a stone in her rear hoof. He was forced to get out of the carriage and ride the other horse but only after assuring himself that both his driver and his mares would be all right, which required a lengthy stop at the nearby ostlers.

Later that afternoon, when Light finally arrived at his Mayfair townhouse, the usually quiet residence was abuzz. Visitors had shown up unannounced. *Visitors?* No one ever came to his lordship's pleasure house. He was told that one of the visitors was quite obviously a lady of quality; as such, her station alone demanded certain niceties; turning a lady away was out of the question. Especially when she'd demanded to see him straight away. *A Lady? Here? Who would call for him here?* This was his pleasure house; it wasn't even listed as one of the residences he owned—only his most trusted staff even knew it existed.

Light took pains to keep this residence a secret. He conducted his official business in his duke's main residence in town square. He made sure that his official and private lives were never interconnected.

He quizzed his butler about the visitors and was told it was an old crone and her grandson both had refused to give their card. He was also told they'd demanded to see him as soon as he arrived. His eyes went wide with shock at hearing that. No one, absolutely no one, ever ordered Lord Light to do anything, let alone an old crone and her yelp.

In the frostiest tone to which he was capable, he informed Bigsby in no uncertain terms were, they to see him immediately. "Let them wait!" He was going to freshen up, take a long bath, shave and have a drink. Once Simon his valet had finished, then and only then would he come down.

"Bigsby If that doesn't suit them, invite them to come back at a more convenient hour. Next week on Tuesday at my mansion in town looks promising."

With that said, he then nonchalantly strode up the stairs, all the while inwardly fuming. *Order me about… in my own home… I think not!*

When he had come down an hour later, looking brilliant in a dark merino wool suit with an expertly tied blue cravat, and crisp white shirt, and gleaming Hessian boots, he was told the old crone had refused to leave and had chosen instead to wait.

"Very well," he spat out.

Frustrated beyond measure, Light ordered them to be shown to his study. He sat in his leather chair, looking as if he didn't have a care in the world, while he watched the old crone shuffle in, leaning heavily on her cane, her gnarled hands trembling. She was escorted by a young dapper, strapping lad in his early twenties whose arrogance evidently matched Light's own. The two men briefly eyed each other, and both found the other lacking.

It was obvious the young pup doted on the old crone as he set her down carefully on the tufted back-wing chair across from Light's desk. The young pup then seated himself close to her.

Without being asked or offered, the young lad picked up Light's tea service and began preparing a cup for the old lady and gently laid it by her elbow. She nodded her thanks to him and smiled indulgently.

Light resisted the urge to roll his eyes. As touching as this domestic scene was, what? He wondered again for the third time, what did any of this have to do with him? But he had learned long ago to have patience, so he waited crossing his long legs watching from lowered eyes. Besides, he knew instinctively when he was in the presence of a lady, and ladies, as a rule, were not to be rushed during their tea.

The crone carefully sipped her tea, and when he was on the verge of asking what he could do for them, she set her teacup down. She leveled her surprisingly clear gray eyes on him and sharply pointed her gnarled fingers at his chest.

"You have my granddaughter hidden in this mausoleum you call a house, and you will produce her here to me this instant. Or I will have the authorities called, and your name dragged through the mud, Light. Do I make myself clear, young man?"

She harrumphed and picked up her tea, took a delicate sip, and then leveled another glare at him when she was finished drinking.

Light was dumbstruck and at a monetary loss for words. No one, that is, no one in all his years, had ever dared talk to him thusly. He was a Duke! He was not sure if someone was playing a joke at this expense, and thus, quite literally, his jaw dropped open. When he realized it was hanging open like a village idiot, he slammed it shut and sat ramrod straight. He checked his memory; had anyone ever had the audacity to talk to him like that? No. He was sure of it. No one ever had, not even his late parents, and he was damned if he would let it start now, let alone by an old bat, in his own home.

"First of all!" he said in a voice louder than he'd intended.

But he never got a chance to finish. The young pup instantly stood up and leveled steely gray eyes on him and then slowly lowered his balled hands one at a time on the imposing desk and eyed light nose to nose in fury.

"I believe," he said through gritted teeth in an ominous voice.

"That I just misheard you. You did not just now raise your voice at my grandmother, did you, LIGHT?"

The last word was growled with such menace that Light was sure a fist would follow it. Not that Light was worried. Let the young pup try if he dared. The young man had barked Light's name as if it was an epithet or a foul curse.

Clearer heads will prevail, Light thought while visibly restraining himself. Still, he decided to find out what was going on here. He looked from the young pup to the old crone and bit back his anger. It was always best to study your enemy, and these two had him at a distinct disadvantage; they knew him, but he didn't know them. They hadn't even had the decency to produce their cards to his butler after arriving at his home uninvited.

Every inch of him longed to swipe that condescending look off the young pup's face, but now was not the time. He had too many unanswered questions. *Who were they? Who was this granddaughter? It's better not be his newest sexual partner, or heads would roll! Did his foolhardy agent secret off some Duke's daughter?* No, that couldn't be, or the guard would be here rather than an old crone and her pup.

Light had always demanded that his partners be willing; he'd never coerced anyone. He was befuddled by this turn of events. But he would get to the bottom of this in time. For now, he had too many unanswered questions.

Chapter Six

Light barely held on to his temper as the pair continued to glower at him. He indicated to the chair across from his desk, and the young pup slowly slid down into it, his back ramrod straight, making it known that he was ready to jump up should any further disrespect be shown to his grandmother.

To buy time, Light went over to his liquor cabinet and brought down his best-malted scotch from the Highlands of Scotland. He poured out two measures for himself, offered one to the pup, and listened to their tale. As the fine scotch burned its way down to his gut, his temper flared even brighter as he listened.

From their tale, Light deduced that they had followed a lead that brought them here from the same hackney driver that had dropped off the young lady yesterday evening. The pair believed that the girl's description matched that of the crone's granddaughter, who had mistakenly been lured to acting as his paramour by some scandalous, unscrupulous means. And they were not leaving until the girl had been fetched and returned to them forthwith.

Light neither admitted nor denied anything as he listened to their tale. Still, he did not like being intimidated, and the threat of authorities in his business could create a real scandal that all his money couldn't erase. The rumors of his clandestine activities already had him on the far outskirts of decent society; only his large pockets and the dukedom kept him within the ton. But he knew better than anyone how unforgiving and fickle society could be. If another juicy scandal broke out like the last one with Patricia, it could be his permanent ruin in polite society. That was far more attention than he wanted on his private affairs. If the girl they were looking for were within the walls of his home, he would return her to them without question and good riddance. Still, she would learn whatever lesson he would deliver to her in the short time he had. She would think twice next time she was tempted to trifle with him or his affairs.

Still, he had too many unanswered questions. *Why had his new partner insisted on double the usual fee and all of it upfront? Had the girl masterminded this entire ruse to get her hands on ten thousand pounds?* It would explain a lot, and it would also explain why she'd wanted to be paid upfront. It occurred to Light that she may have even sent the old crone and her grandson. *Was this some sort of blackmail on his affairs?* But judging by the quality of the clothes on the pair in his study, they were gentry and high gentry at that. The old lady carried herself like a duchess, though an aged one. Her clothes were costly and well made, however, dated. It was unlikely she needed ten thousand pounds, and she didn't seem the sort to go to these lengths to get it. Yes, there were still too many unanswered questions. Only the girl could answer them all, and he had yet to meet her acquaintance-no time like the present.

"What is the girl's first name?" he inquired blandly, as if they were discussing the weather.

"Her name is Samantha," said the young pup insolently with a dare in his eyes. It seemed he was daring Light to deny she was here.

Light was dying to wipe that arrogant smirk off the pup's face, but now was not the time. Soon, he promised himself. Soon.

Light rose, intent on questioning the girl that had brought so much chaos to his usually tranquil residence. As he stood up, questions continued to plague him. *Was this some lark by an overindulged, bored aristocratic girl?* He had no idea, but whoever this Miss Samantha was, she would rue the day she decided to tangle with him and his affairs.

With that grim thought, he excused himself from the sour-faced dowager and her pup. All the excitement he had felt earlier at meeting his newest acquisition dried up in his gut like dust. *Would he have to give up his newest sexual partner?* All roads seemed to point in that direction, but at least the young lady involved would pay some small penance of her own for this afternoon's devilment. He would see to it. He would scare her so thoroughly that she would never again conceive of becoming a thorn in his side!

As he walked out of the study, he again wondered if she had concocted this scheme as a quick means to get ten thousand pounds. His mood was positively sour when he ordered the young lady to be summoned to him. He wanted to talk to her privately, and he wanted the truth.

"Place her in my underground playroom."

He ordered his footman.

The man was a credit to the role he was hired for; he was discreet, and he never blinked, just followed instructions quickly and efficiently.

Light never used the underground dungeon playroom any more. He had experimented with it more in his younger days, when his sexual tastes had run darker and when the loss of both of his parents still tormented him. His despair at losing both his parents had so haunted him that he'd turned to sex as a means of escape—the darker the sex, the better. But in time, he had grown bored with it, preferring the simple pleasures he could have in the upstairs bedrooms instead. But today, he felt its oppressive atmosphere would serve his purpose. He intended to disabuse the young lady of her desire to ever meddle with his affairs again.

It was an intimidating room, and it was structured for just that purpose. It was an actual dungeon that he'd inherited as part of his holdings, and he'd converted it for his purposes. The stairs leading to it were dark and dank, and it was so far below the rest of the house that no sounds from the dungeon could be heard on the main floor. The heavy double-bolted gray door was braced with handmade iron, and the ancient scones provided little light. The inside playroom was no less oppressive; gray, cold brick blocks lined the floor and walls, and dark, dangerous-looking ancient weapons hung on the wall next to heavy metal chains.

Chapter Seven

Light sat at his desk in his underground dungeon, his anger building. He was facing the south wall, so he didn't see the girl when she entered, escorted by a discreet footman. Without turning around, he told his footman to place her in the inspection area and leave quickly. He heard her sit in the wooden chair and purposely ignored her for several long minutes. Let her sweat, he thought angrily, knowing how hot the candle chandelier lights were above her head. He'd had the chandelier custom made, and it held over a hundred large wax candles.

After a lengthy silence, he then heard a chair being dragged away from the hot lights; she seemed to want respite from the heat in the inspection area.

"Do not move!" he barked.

"Do not move anything in this room unless I specifically tell you to do so. Do you understand me!"

He turned then and stumbled when he saw her. The affect her beauty had on him was unexpected and instantaneous. He leaned heavily on the oak desk for support.

He was grateful that the room was dimmed on his end so that she didn't see his immediate reaction on his first glimpse of her. His first thought was that she was stunning. His second thought was, what the hell had Gordon Allen had been thinking?

Of course, the old lady and her grandson had come for her. *Who wouldn't come for her?* She was exquisite. She was tall for a lady, slender and voluptuous. Her hair and face were elegant, refined, and innocent. His hand itched to run his fingers through her waist-length silky locks which flowed around her in rich waves.

If she were his, he'd never let her leave his sight, and if she were missing, he would roam the ends of the earth looking for her (just like the old croon and her arrogant yelp!). But something about her caught his attention even further than her beauty, and he couldn't quite put his finger on it. She sat perfectly still, unruffled, under the hot chandelier lights.

He was surprised now to find that she didn't appear to be afraid of him at all. For one so young, she sat stiffly and made direct eye contact with him. She seemed to consider him an equal. Intriguing. A calm intelligence hovered behind her eyes, it saw through him, assessed him, and at length it retreated behind a serene mask of cluelessness. It all happened so fast he almost doubted it had happened at all. Shaken, he tried and failed to recover his gruff mien.

"What is your name?"

He asked in a loud voice. He was annoyed, half hoping that it wasn't the girl they were looking for. For this girl was truly stunning, and he already longed to spend the time he'd contracted for with her. He wanted very much to get to know her better. He wanted very much to retain the feelings her presence was stirring within him. Her assessing look had given him something he'd never even known he wanted—she saw through him. In just a brief moment, she'd seen past all the bluster of his title, his social standing, his political connections—seen through all that—to the man within. He was seen, and it was liberating. He sensed that she didn't particularly like what she saw in him, but that was an issue for another day. Today he was seen. It puzzled him why that small fact made him feel less lonely. And where had she retreated to. He didn't like the mask that was now firmly in place looking back at him coldly and with detachment. How could he get past that mask? But he would never get his chance. She was retreating even further.

He noticed suddenly that something had caught her attention. She was studying the details of the room, one by one, and her aloofness was fast fading as color slowly drained from her face. *This was what he had intended, wasn't it?* But now that he had met her, he wasn't quite so sure about this approach. He definitely wasn't as pleased with the outcome it was having on her as he'd thought he would be. In fact, he was chagrined; he wished he could start all over again and never bring her here at all.

She carefully studied the various whips, chains, and manacles above the fireplace in the dungeon. She then looked in consternation at the artwork on the walls, all depicting a female in various states of undress being whipped by different instruments such as leather belts and wooden paddles. In one picture, the male had a leather leash around a girl's neck, and the girl was being walked like a dog on all fours while dressed in very revealing clothes.

"Samantha," she said, at last, turning to face him coldly, her face pale and her back became even straighter.

So, it was her. Her voice was surprising, it sent tingles along his spine. It was throaty but musical, at the same time, seductive. Her eyes were as clear as a lake, and he found it difficult to imagine that she was capable of any artifice. He instantly memorized her face; her image became etched in his brain. He was drawn to her in a way that surprised him.

However, Light was even further annoyed by his body's reaction to her. This little slip of a girl made him feel uncomfortable, and she glowed with an inner light that shone right thru her iridescent skin. She looked so pure but enticing and voluptuous all at the same time. He regretted losing her even before he'd had her.

He wanted to claim some small part of her, exert his dominance over her before letting her go. She seemed so aloof and so untouchable—so calm despite her consternation at the oppressive room, he walked over to her and looked her over carefully. Her clear eyes met his without flinching. *An equal (he instantly recognized her to be that).* He knew an equal when he met one. *But how? She was younger, she was a female, and according to their agreement, he was the master and outside of that agreement he outranked her—he was a duke.* He was momentarily at a loss, then his anger resurfaced unreasonably, and he grabbed her roughly and kissed her full on the mouth. Her lips didn't move. They lay still and pliant beneath his, and he realized belatedly that she had never been kissed before. A strange exultation filled him, and he pulled back his force and lightly pressed into her lips again this time guiding, instructing, pleading. She didn't respond. Then in time, she slowly mimicked his movements.

After a while, he gentled his hold on her and angled his face over her, running his tongue over her lower lip and then further into her mouth. At last, her tongue met his and as she returned the kiss, his body instantly reacted. The reaction was so swift and violet he felt dizzy it was so different from anything that he had ever experienced. He pulled her closer to him just to be sure that he hadn't imagined it, and sure enough, that spark within was still there and it grew. She tasted sweeter and purer than anything he had ever tasted in all his adult life. All the dark sexual desires that had consumed him so thoroughly for decades fled as if they had never existed. She made him feel like any ordinary gentleman with a beautiful girl in his arms; an airy giddiness filled his loins. He pressed his fullness against her skirts enjoying the friction and the inappropriateness of his actions.

He released her, and she swayed, unsteadily. He studied her quietly. Then his first genuine smile of the evening filled his lips.

Chapter Eight

"Well, Samantha," he said languidly.

"It seems our acquaintance is to be cut short even before it began. Your grandmother and a young man are here to collect you."

Relief flooded her features, and it was then that he truly realized how young she was. He saw what a strain the last few moments had put on her, though he would never have known it from all her bravado. He found himself getting momentarily lost in her hazel eyes, which were now filled with relief. He saw that she was very happy to be seeing the last of him, not that he blamed her, he reflected wryly. He had made an especially poor first impression. Not entirely by design.

"I pride myself on my discretion, Miss Samantha. No one need ever know you were here, and I would like your word that no one will know anything of what you have seen here today." He moved his eyes meaningfully around the room.

"Yes, My Lord," she said.

"You have my word."

That look of relief was still there about her features, and it was starting to annoy him. She needn't look for all the world as if she had escaped the hangman's noose. *He wasn't an ogre, after all, was he?*

In an attempt to wipe that look off from her face, he said, "There is still that matter of the ten thousand pounds that your family now owes me. I would ask that you all do me the honor of joining me for dinner tonight so that we can discuss it."

Samantha nodded slowly. She looked like she wanted to flee from him, and the oppressive room post haste, but she was too gently bred to do so. She waited until he dismissed her. A strange ache started to build in Lord Light's heart. She was light, and he was dark, despite his name. The misnomer light had been given to him by his chums as a joke. But she had real light, and it had started to spill over to him, showing him a loneliness within himself that he hadn't even known existed. In their short kiss, she had begun to fill that hole, and now she was leaving. He felt uncharacteristically bereft, an emotion he was sure he had never felt before. All of a sudden, he felt every one of his years—all five and thirty of them.

He nodded to the door, and to her credit, Samantha walked calmly to the dungeon door, pulling it open with effort and closing it heavily behind her. And when the door closed, he heard her fast footfalls rush up the stairs as quickly as her body could carry her. She ran as if the hounds of hell were chasing her. And maybe they were. *Maybe they were.*

Chapter Nine

Samantha was not too ashamed to bury her head in her grandmama's lap as soon as she entered her bedchambers. Her grandmama had been placed in the same room assigned to Samantha at their mutual request, and Bart was placed in a bed chamber across the hall. They all were to wait in their rooms until dinner. Grandmama had argued that they would not be staying for dinner but would be leaving forthwith. But his lordship's butler had insisted.

"It's too dark and too late to travel now, my lady," Bigsby, had fumed uncharacteristically flustered.

"His Lordship doesn't want to risk your safety on such a long journey especially since we've received reports of highwaymen about."

"You are now under the protection of the Liechfield name. We beg you to accept our hospitality for one night, we will endeavor to make you as comfortable as the queen, I promise."

The old butler was as feisty as grandmama, and in the end, she'd agreed to accept the lord's hospitality, unwanted though it was.

Samantha had never been so glad to have her family close to her as she was tonight. Bart joined her and grandmama in Samatha's room as he grilled her.

"What in all that is holy had you been thinking of to end up here?"

Here!

He shouted, incredulously looking about as if he were in hell itself. She confessed to eavesdropping on the conversation in the study, and, as a result, she'd done all this to save her family. For a solid hour, both Bart and Grandmere berated her soundly for her actions. But in the end, they were just glad that she was safe and that they had arrived in time before anything could transpire between her and Light.

Even though she was still ruined. Grandmama held out some hope, however small, that no one of consequence had seen an unescorted, unmarried young woman enter a gentleman's bachelor residence alone and stay for an entire night.

"One can only hope," whispered Grandmere, twisting her gnarled hands in consternation as she paced in the large room: pondering her granddaughters' ruination.

An hour later, Samantha primped self-consciously before the large looking glass mirror, grand-mama, and Bart had already gone to dinner. She needed a minute by herself. She still trembling from the encounter she'd had with Lord "Light" that "afternoon." *To think that she'd signed up for six months of that!* How could she have even endured six days, when just one meeting with him had shaken her up to the core. *And that awful room!* She shuddered uncontrollably, remembering the dark scenes on the dank dungeon wall; her best poker face had barely gotten her through.

Her thoughts, unbidden, went back again and again to Lord Light. She'd never seen a man so beautiful and strong. But he had to be the devil himself. The painted images on his walls had her face turning scarlet. The images depicted a level of cruelty that she couldn't reconcile with the upper classes (many of whom considered themselves too dignified to interact with any of the members of the lower classes). Weren't the lower classes the ones that were labeled animalistic and crude. How could a gentleman of his level—a duke—no less take pleasure in such open barbarism? As a well-bred lady's daughter, she certainly hadn't ever seen anything like it, nor did she ever want to again. She was not only shocked to within an inch of her life, but she was also badly shaken by the experience, even two hours later. The images in her mind's eye of whips, chains, and constraints applied to innocent female flesh tore at her. Along with the dominating atmosphere (it had chilled her). Her usual serenity had not sufficed to win the day. Thus, she'd dug deep into her soul, and thankfully, a deep calm had surrounded her, allowing her to see to the innermost depths of the scary gentleman before her. She'd been surprised to see beneath all his bluster was a very alienated, very lonely little boy inside the huge man. She saw someone that had been scared most of his life and as a result, built scary things around him to scare off others. For just a moment, they'd both seen each other as they really were (seen past the pretense and the bluster). Neither had been ready nor prepared for the shock that "seeing" would cause. So, they'd carried on as if nothing was amiss. Similar to a Hackney driver that dies in a bad carriage accident but doesn't accept the death; he carries on to pick up other passengers as if the death had never happened. A deep connection had been forged by the two of them in that dungeon, but neither had been ready to accept it; they'd carried on as if nothing had happened.

Physically, he hadn't hurt her in that confounding interlude; he was after all, a gentleman (*of sorts*). But what he'd exposed her eyes to was mind-shattering, considering her sheltered existence (and that kiss—it had been pure bliss). She hadn't been prepared for the effect of that kiss on her senses. She had melted into his arms (once she'd learned what to do that is)… her first kiss!

She'd never expected her first kiss to be like that. Involuntarily, she kept thinking of him. He was so beautiful and yet so naughty, yet lonely. Something about him drew her (against her wishes, she didn't want to like him, she didn't want to be attracted to him, she didn't want anything to do with him). He was sin personified, tall, dark, and handsome, with hair as black as midnight slicked back perfectly in place. He was also trim and powerful; his rock-hard physique had been well outlined in his finely tailored clothes. A part of her had wanted to reach out and touch that chiseled stone physique and feel it melt under her hands.

She tried to block out his image from her mind's eye as she carefully dressed for dinner. She had to admit that the new clothes that Sophie had made for her showed off her figure and coloring to perfection. She didn't know why, but she wanted to look her best. Tonight, she wore a yellow satin evening gown. It cleverly hugged her voluptuous figure while remaining elegant and modest. The underskirt flowed around her hips in rich waves of a darker yellow satin that complemented the bodice. Tiny diamond studs peaked out in neat rows in a bodice that tightly hugged her bosom, drawing attention to her enticing feminine shape. She had to admit that she looked even more stunning than usual. She loved how the new designs allowed her to feel luxurious while allowing her to be extremely modest; as a girl that had never officially come out, she was limited in the designs she was allowed to wear. With her mother's diamond jewels complementing the ensemble, she looked every inch the lady of good breeding that she was. Her cheeks bloomed all on their own from this afternoon's indecent activities, but it was an understatement to say that she wasn't nervous to see Light again.

She longed to confide in someone but with all her friends moved away and now Healey gone; Bart was the only confident she had left, and she couldn't confide in him (not any more and not about this).

Bart, Healey, and she had been true confidantes at one point, never hiding anything from each other. The three friends had made a childhood vow to always tell each other the truth. They were as thick as thieves growing up, despite their obvious differences in station. Even though Healey was their servant, they'd all grown up together, and stations had ceased to matter (especially in the country where proprieties were a little more relaxed). Besides, the three friends had been united, in their hate of the old governess, the warthog. They'd gotten each other into and out of more scrapes than their governess could count. It was perhaps due to all of their rigorous, mischievous endeavors that the governess had decided to take an early permanent retirement, never to be seen or heard from again. But now Bart was no longer himself, and neither was Healey. Bart had returned from Eton unexpectedly one day and never went back. He'd quickly become a cold, unapproachable man; gone was the warm, beloved brother she'd always adored. It had been evident he was drowning under some heavy grief, but he'd refused to unburden himself and confide in her. Samantha missed their prior close camaraderie. In many ways, she missed Bart the most out of all the people she'd lost. Perhaps it was because he was still alive but just as lost to her as those that had passed away. She longed to confide in him, but every time she tried, he put up a wall. And worse, he now treated her like a naïve child. That stung the most because, in their childhood, he'd given her the nickname of "Boss" out of his respect for her immense mischievous intellect. He'd called her "Boss" even though she was younger than him and a female; by rights, as heir apparent, he could have claimed that title for himself, but he hadn't. Instead, he'd followed her leadership in their schemes. She'd loved him for that. Where everyone else eschewed her intelligence, Bart had been the only one to welcome it. As such, he had been the only person she could truly be herself around. But not any more, even though she couldn't confide in him about this afternoon's trying events, she was still glad he was here. His presence would help get her through this dinner with Light. She felt lucky that both her family members were here tonight. Head held high, she took a deep, fortifying breath and went downstairs to dinner, her impassive poker face firmly in place.

*

Light had taken advantage of the afternoon's respite to discipline his agent. Gordon Allen was punished for his reckless behavior with a hefty deduction of his usual fee. Light demanded to know everything Gordon knew about the girl and her family.

By the time Light dressed for dinner, he felt he had a closer grasp of the facts of what had led the girl to such a rash action. He had personally spoken to a few of her creditors that were able to make time to see him on such short notice. The dukedom had its advantages. After these hasty meetings, he realized that the family was in dire straits; they needed someone with deep pockets such as his to climb out of the hole they were in. His further digging around had also shown that the grandmother had a good and ancient title and that she was not willing to sacrifice the girl's happiness to save the family from ruin by marrying her off to save their home. The grandmother wanted a true love match for her only granddaughter, who she doted on. Light could believe that from the way the old termagant had come at him earlier today. He should be glad to be rid of the whole mess of them. But he couldn't, in good conscience, let them travel unaccompanied to their home some many days' ride away in the middle of the night when highwaymen were about. He'd succor them for one night. By tomorrow, they all would be someone else's problem.

He pounded his chest again, that odd pain filling him ever since he'd kissed the girl. The thought of saying goodbye to her brought ambivalent feelings, some good/ some bad.

Come on, old man!

He admonished his reflection in the mirror. *What's one chit out of so many in the world? And it's not as if she'd have you anyway, not for all the gold in the kingdom. You've seen to that.* He chuckled to himself, remembering how she'd fled his presence as if the hounds of hell were chasing her. That was probably how she saw him. Someone as innocent as her had no business dealing with someone as tainted as him. It was all for the best that they parted ways now. *Wasn't it?*

Chapter Ten

That thought served him in good stead until he saw her again that evening in the great hall. He stopped mid-stride on his way to the sitting room and studied her surreptitiously before any of the guests knew he had arrived. His body reacted immediately to the sight of her. Exquisite! She was exquisite. *How is it she hadn't been married off before now?* Even without a title, any number of lords would have thrown in their caps for her.

He blinked despite himself at how absolutely stunning she was, and without making a conscious decision, he decided that he had to have her. He now cursed the impulse that had caused him to bring her to that dark playroom in the dungeon. Now her defenses would be doubly barred against him.

He proceeded on with his host duties, doing his best to make her family feel welcome in his home. While they all waited for dinner in the main sitting room, he studied her through hooded dark gray eyes while casually trying to make inane conversation with her family.

"How are you this fine evening, he asked the grandmother." No response.

"I hope the accommodations are acceptable," he persisted pleasantly. Again, no response.

They made it clear they did not like him, nor did they want to converse with him. Her grandmother was tight-lipped and silent. She sat ramrod straight in his King Louis VIII leather tufted chair, looking like a deposed monarch and an unhappy one at that. Samantha's brother leaned casually against the marble fireplace, making ready with Light's best scotch, and looking as if he wanted to pound Light into the ground with his bare hands! He also was silent.

Samantha, to her credit, sat calmly on the settee, looking like any warmly invited guest into the home of a close friend. She smiled easily, and when no one else answered Light's attempts at conversation, she supplied a ready answer. She was self-possessed, confident, and warm, but not cloying. Unlike most females of Light's acquaintance, she didn't seem particularly impressed that he was a duke. 'You've seen one duke, you've seen them all,' seemed to be her demeanor.

She wore a stunning confection of yellow satin that complemented her translucent skin and matched the brownish-yellow flecks in her clear hazel eyes. Her hair was a startling display of blonde colors, almost shimmering and very thick. It was styled in a smart chignon on the side of her head, with long wisps framing her face. This combination of colors would have looked washed out on anyone else, but since she had such prominent cheekbones and long dark brown lashes and brows, it all came together as striking, and Light was hard-pressed to take his eyes off her. He alternately cursed and applauded Gordon Allen.

The butler announced that dinner was ready, but Light wasn't given the option to escort either lady to the main dining room. Samantha's brother promptly bowed at both ladies, and one took his right arm and the other his left arm. Light was left to follow the trio as they made their way to dinner. Everyone seemed to forget that he was the ranking peer and that it was his home.

The tension at dinner was no less intense, though the food

was superb. The staff served noodle soup with croquettes as a starter. The next seven courses included Parisienne potatoes, filet of pompano, roasted quail, sweet bread pate, venison stew, and French peas. They ended with a delicious plum pudding, assorted cakes, Debrie cheese, and coffee. Champagne flowed ceaselessly throughout the meal. On par with the excellent food were the staff and their presentation of the meal.

Nevertheless, Samantha barely ate. The apprehension in the room was so thick one could cut it with a knife. She breathed a sigh of relief when the meal was almost concluded. The strain of keeping up all the polite conversation through all seven courses by herself had started to show.

Grandmere and Bart had been void of emotion during the entire interminable meal, with Bart only breaking the silence to ask for more scotch.

During the last course, the Duke dismissed the staff and asked for privacy. Bart looked up at Light with a cocked eyebrow and a challenging look in his hazel eyes. Light put up both hands in the air as if to say, hear me out.

"I think we started out on the wrong foot," he said to no one in particular. "I'm no fool, and I know what I'm about to say should be said in a closed room with just you and I."

He looked directly at Bart.

"But I know that you wouldn't give anything I have to say the slightest consideration. You feel that I have placed a slur on your sister's reputation, but I'm asking to have my say here, in front of the ladies, because I feel, in part, it is Samantha's decision to make, and I'd like you all to be present. If you all would please step into my study."

He motioned to the door.

Bart looked as if he would like nothing better than to call

Light out, swords or pistols drawn at dawn, but he gave a jerky nod of his dark head and rose stiffly. He escorted his sister and grandmother to Light's study, one lady on each arm, not allowing Light to touch either of his relations. He carefully seated each of them across from Lights desk and stood behind them in a protective stance. Light indicated a third chair, but Bart shook his head, he preferred to stand. Light closed and locked the door with a distinctive clink, and everyone waited silently while Light seated himself carefully and then began speaking.

Light took another deep breath, feeling like the weight of all he stood for hung in the balance. He wasn't sure why he felt thusly, but he suddenly felt like it was the most important thing on earth that he made his points correctly. Sometimes a man's whole future rested on a few key decisions, and this was just such a moment. He knew only that he had to have her. He looked at Samantha's face and then her grandmother's wooden stare, and he faltered but soon regained his resolve. Taking a deep breath, he began to speak.

Chapter Eleven

"In light of the misunderstanding that has brought you all here, I would like to make a fresh start. In the short time I have made your acquaintance." He looked at Samantha.

"Which was just today."

He clarified for her brother in case they thought he had already ruined the girl, but in the eyes of the ton, anytime a woman spent in a single man's house without a chaperone was ruination, so his speech on that topic was just semantics.

"Again, that was just today," he repeated in a note of rare nervousness.

He cleared his throat and moved on. Why was he so nervous? The feeling was foreign to him. He had made an untold number of speeches in parliament in front of dignitaries from all over the world without batting an eyelash but now his hands were shaking. He began again.

"By a fresh start, I mean I would like to press my suit for marriage."

The room was silent.

"I understand if my suit is not accepted, but I would at least like it to be considered before it is turned down out of hand. To show my good faith, if my suit is accepted, I would agree to a betrothal contract that would settle the sum of 100,000 thousand pounds on my betrothed."

"The girl is not for sale!" The grandmother piped up, banging her cane once for good measure.

"I have your measure, Light." She squinted in his direction. "I've done my homework on you."

Light looked at Samantha, but she was silent. He looked to Bart, who was also silent. They were closing ranks and closing him out.

They had weighed him, measured him, and found him wanting. *Did they then?* He was not used to that feeling. And the sentiment that feeling invoked within him caused the uncomfortable stirrings in his chest to return. He unconsciously rubbed his pectoral muscle. He wasn't quite sure they were wrong about him. He wasn't perfect, far from it, in fact.

He looked at Samantha again. Something within her called out to him. It pierced through his pride, and he tried again. He knew he had been more than generous, and he also knew they needed the money. But it was his reputation that had stopped them, and he hadn't done himself any favors by bringing Samantha to that playroom. Check, mate. He'd outsmarted himself. But Light was made of sterner stuff than that, especially when it came to something he really wanted, and he wanted her.

He began again.

"Of course," he persisted.

"I would ask for a betrothal period of at least one month. If my bride-to-be decides to break off the engagement after that time, she will keep the money, and I wouldn't press my suit any further. Let's all keep in mind that a betrothal would also safeguard Samantha's reputation."

No one physically moved, but Light felt the energy in the room shift. He had a chance, however small, at the angel in the yellow dress. To win her, he would have to move heaven and earth and do it all in thirty days. He was a master at moving earth—that much he knew. The trouble was that he had no knowledge of how to move heaven. But he wanted to learn. He was shocked to realize just how much he wanted to learn, especially if it gave him a chance at Samantha.

"I'll leave you all to discuss in private," he said firmly.

"I'll be in my library. If you need me, Bigsby, my butler can fetch me from there. Just ring for him."

He bowed to Samantha and her grandma and left the room.

Chapter Twelve

It was midnight before the family finished discussing the *"situation."*

They agreed to the betrothal, as Light knew they would. He could tell by the tough terms of the contract that the old crone had dictated them. They would allow him thirty days of courtship—no more; the entire courtship would take place at Evansdale Manor under the watchful eye of Samantha's family. To mind proprieties, they would host a house party so that it would be proper for him to be in their home for an extended time. The family also demanded half of the money upfront and that Samantha be properly chaperoned at all times.

They also demanded the right to have other suitors present to compete for Samantha's hand so that she could choose the best love match for herself. The family insisted on their own solicitor reviewing the details of the betrothal contract, and they would respond within the week.

The thirty days would begin once Light arrived at Evansdale Manor, and he was asked to bring one relative to the house party who would vouch for his honor. He was also informed that the betrothal wouldn't be announced until the end of the thirty days at the final ball. All the other suitors would also be invited to the ball and house party.

Light was no fool; he insisted on a few conditions of his own, but by and by, the deal was struck. It was just up to the solicitors to draft it and finish it up.

*

Light whistled a merry tune as he made his way to his bed later that night. Although he had just agreed to give away a bloody fortune, he couldn't remember feeling this happy in years. *But where in the hell would he find one relative to vouch for his honor? Oh well, he was sure he could dig one up somewhere.* He drifted off to sleep with memories of Samantha's kiss filling his mind.

*

A week later, late at night in his main residence, Light frowned into his scotch. For once, the deep satisfying color and smooth burn did not ease his body in the slightest. All of his muscles were rigid with an inexplicable tautness, and his nerves felt stretched almost to the point of pain.

He half-listened to the domestic sounds all around him as the servants prepared for bed. Everything around him was peaceful, nothing accounted for the unbearable tension in his body. Nothing, that is, but his thoughts.

The whole house was settling in for the night. He heard the muted steps of the footmen as they went about their evening duties. His butler had already retired, and with a gentle tap on the library door, Rigsby had entered the study with his master's nightly libation on a small tray.

"Will that be all, sir?" he'd asked, his sonorous voice followed by a lift of his perfectly trimmed brow.

At that exact moment, the huge grandfather clock in the sunroom had rung nine times. His butler was nothing if not timely. Light waved a dismissive hand, too lost in thought to respond.

Now, almost three hours later, he sat in the same place where Bigsby had left him, a victim of his own thoughts. The room was dim, the candles were turned off, and a roaring fire in the grill was the only light in the spacious room. Lord Light had his back to the fire, looking with unseeing eyes out the library window at shapes in the garden. He didn't like to admit it, but he was unable to switch his mind off from the girl. How vexing for a man who prided himself on being so jaded. He was cynical to a fault. So cynical, in fact, that even the most fantastic ladies at Miss Jansbell's House of Rare Beauties evoked in him only a mild interest. It took a beauty who was skilled at his more risqué pleasures to evoke in him a true desire in him, and even then, it was fleeting. So, fleeting as to last only a few weeks at best, and even then, the inevitable ennui would return in its full force. *What in the world would it take to be permanently enamored with a woman like his mates all were?*

He sometimes wondered why he'd never fallen in love. He'd always assumed that he was just immune to cupid's pull, be that as it may, he enjoyed his carefree lifestyle. His only irritation was that he longed for an attraction that would last at least a few months, or failing that, he'd settle for one that lasted until past the fast-breaking.

Now he sat in the peculiar position of being unable to shake off thoughts of a mere girl from his mind and knowing that, because of his impudence, she thoroughly abhorred him. He would have liked to explore her and her unusual effect on him in languor. Till now, he'd scrupulously avoided virgin maidens, finding them too innocent and too childish for his tastes. Yet somehow Samantha's calm features affected him differently.

It was novel for him to be this intrigued by any beauty. His analytical mind wanted to get to the root of this bizarre attraction. But how to do it when she had fled from him hell for leather as far away as she could get? Her defenses were high against him, and if that wasn't obstacle enough, the young pup and old crone that protected her with a fanatical loyalty would close ranks against him faster than a crow could walk on a grave.

He licked his full, firm lips in consternation. That action invoked in him an image of Samantha as she had been, in his arms, in that horrid training room. The contradiction of her innocence in such a room of dark pleasure had been intoxicating. It was like witnessing a mating between light and dark. She'd looked and tasted like pure sunlight. Her skin had even glowed with some internal luminosity all its own. She'd looked so natural and wholesome as if she'd swallowed the sun, looking ethereal under those harsh lights. Yet he'd sensed a strength in her. In the way she'd stared back at him with her delicate features not flinching, and her head held high (regal, aloof, untouchable).

He'd never admit it, even under torture, but her finesse and strength in the face of that harsh dungeon had earned his grudging admiration. After she'd left, he'd looked at the sexual scenes depicted in the artwork in that room with new eyes, and he'd been slightly ashamed of himself.

While in the room, she'd seemed so cold and unreachable. Ultimately, that's why he'd kissed her; he'd wanted to dominate her, possess her, brand her, and breach her defenses. But at best, that skirmish had been a draw. Her touch had both burned and warmed him in turn, and in truth, he'd been the one branded and possessed. Even now, a week later, places in him that he hadn't even known existed still seemed to hum with a strange yearning for her.

Light scoffed at himself. *Good God, was he going soft over a chit?* No, he shook his head vehemently; he was just in need of a good bedding. But the trajectory of his thoughts concerned him as his focus repeatedly went back to her. *What was next in this bizarre menagerie of thoughts parading around in his brain? Was he next to spout useless poetry in her honor?*

God forbid!

He slammed his drink down. Damn the chit. He didn't need her, and he didn't want her.

That last untruth gave him pause. Even in his jaded state, he still recognized the truth. And the truth was that his desire for her was unmatched. He wanted her. In fact, he wanted her more than he'd wanted anything in a long time, and when Light wanted something, Light got it. The consequences be damned.

He stared at the signed betrothal contract on his desk. He'd gotten confirmation days ago that it had been signed by both solicitors and that the 50,000 pounds and his late mother's betrothal ring had been delivered to the girl at Evansdale Manor. It was with all these troubling thoughts in his mind that he began to further the plan he'd put into motion with the chit's family. He was going to win her if it was the last thing he did. He pulled out several sheets of parchment and his ink pot and penned several missives.

Chapter Thirteen

Several hours later, Light was in his carriage on the way to her family estate, much to the annoyance of his valet, his butler, and his entire household staff. He'd roused the household at the ungodly hour of three a.m. and demanded that arrangements be made forthwith for his imminent travel to the countryside. He couldn't be persuaded to put off going to her for another minute. His butler had come as close to a reprimand as he'd ever given in a score of years.

"If it is your wish, your Grace, to wake up the entire household in this chaotic fashion at this ungodly hour, then I will do so."

"I will rouse them forthwith from their beds."

He'd drawled with no small measure of annoyance creasing his lofty features.

"Yes, Bigsby, that is exactly my wish, and do be quick about it, old man."

Light added with an unusually broad grin, somehow happy to needle the old goat. Not that he got any response from Bigsby for his trouble.

Light felt as if he were on the edge of a grand adventure, and some unused childlike spirit in him was enjoying every moment of it.

Bigsby bowed stiffly and, with a great show of long-suffering, he departed to wake up the household staff and ordered the carriage brought around for his master's looming travel to the countryside. Despite being put out, Bigsby outdid himself. In his usual perfectionist style, everything was pulled off first class, even in the rather short time frame.

Lord Light was now gingerly dozing in a well-fitted carriage with a soft cashmere wool blanket around his hips, a large basket of food in the seat beside him, and a warm tin of tea beside it. To his immense delight, as he dozed off in the well-sprung carriage, on his way to Evansdale, the girl in the yellow dress came to him in his dreams. Her skin, soft like velvet, she wrapped her arms around him, and he dreamt of all the ways he would tutor her in the art of pleasing a man, her aloof features swimming up to him in the memory of his consciousness. The power of the dream kept him in a restful slumber way longer than was his usual style. As such, he arrived at Evansdale energetic, refreshed, and ready to begin his courtship.

Chapter Fourteen

Samantha was filled with awe as she walked through Evansdale Manor. Their once shabby-looking estate was now proud and elegant, its former glory restored. In just a few short weeks, most of the old staff had been rehired, and they now worked tirelessly day and night to return the estate back to her former splendor before the guests arrived.

Grandmama was in rare form; she was ecstatic at the clever deal she had worked out for her only granddaughter. Samantha would get the betrothal funds Light had promised, they would save Evansdale and use some of the funds as Samantha's dowry after the engagement with Light ended. Neither lady would have to deal with that foul Light, but under the expertly negotiated terms of the contract, they would still get to keep his money. She cackled in glee to herself, a rare broad grin filling her lined face.

Grandmama had the fifty percent deposit of Light's funds in her hands, she had received it the week prior. Using those funds, she'd paid off most of the creditors, bought back their family heirlooms, and ordered a fine trousseau for Samantha. She'd significantly updated her granddaughter's wardrobe to ensure that Samantha looked elegant and refined for the upcoming house party. At the end of the house party, a ball was planned for all the guests. Invitations had been sent out to the creme de la creme of elite society, and everyone who was anyone had accepted. Most had accepted out of sheer morbid curiosity, as they were absolutely astounded that the family had made such a remarkable comeback from the brink of poverty. *How did they do it?* The wagging tongues were all agog, many angling for invitations to the house party just so they would be the first to get the scoop and spread the gossip.

But Grandmama's memory was long; she knew who had stood with her family in their time of trouble and who hadn't. She had some things in store for the ton when all this was behind them. She was a believer that revenge was a dish best served in courses. Excluding certain close friends that longed for an invitation was her first course of revenge. More of her retaliations would be delivered incrementally until each one of her nemeses had eaten their own liver, as it were over several courses.

In the meantime, Grand Mere prepared Samantha for her reintroduction into polite society. She was meticulous in showing off her granddaughter to her best advantage. First by providing her the best seamstress, then an expert cobbler, and lastly, hiring a new personal French maid with an incredible talent for hair and clothing.

She doted on her adorable granddaughter. She had worked tirelessly to ensure that her only granddaughter had a secure future. Especially because Samantha didn't have a title, as such she needed Samantha to marry well. With that in mind, Grand Mere had groomed Samantha to be an accomplished lady since leading strings. Training her to stand out in other ways, her carriage, manner of dress, teaching her household management, music instruction, embroidery, painting, and equestrian skills. Her dowry had been a big draw in the past to attract suitors. Evansdale Manor was entailed to Bart. However, Grandmere ensured that Samantha wouldn't arrive at her marriage contract penniless, thanks to the dowry she'd create from Light's monies. But it wouldn't be as large a dowry as Samantha had previously.

Samanatha would still need a suitor that didn't need a title or a large dowry. That was a tall order indeed. Grandmama had invited only those lords that fit that bill, mostly second sons of the gentry, wealthy widowers, select merchants, and independently wealthy members of the peerage.

Tomorrow Samantha's erstwhile fiancé, Light, would arrive, but even his daunting presence did not diminish Grandmama's happiness.

*

Samantha inspected everything in the grand house; all their fine heirlooms were back in their place of glory. Fine art, priceless statues, tall vases from the orient, and even the priceless Louis XV gold-encrusted plates from France were back in their place of honor on the dining table. She had to admit the mansion looked stunning; fine tapestries gleamed and shone, and everywhere that had previously been bare winked with elegant touches. The vast estate was shown to perfection, and all the previously closed wings were open, aired, and brightened. They were now ready to host the king himself. The Minnis family was back, and she felt pride that her estate looked so grand. It was as if the troubles of the past few years had never been.

Chapter Fifteen

The wonderful smells from the kitchen were overwhelming. Samantha as the smell of baked pheasant, roasted lamb, and fresh bread filled the hallways. She only wished that Healey was here, but it had not been possible to get her back.

She left the main hall to go inspect the indoor trees. She looked at her elegant reflection in the tall-looking glass inside the orangery. Sunlight streamed in from the sunroom, and a flood of light fell over the tall orange trees in the greenhouse. This had always been her favorite room in the mansion; it always smelled so wonderful. There was a beautiful life-size statue of Mother Mary in supplication, and a small indoor pond flowed peacefully from Mary to the indoor trees.

After kneeling at the statue and saying a quick prayer, Samantha again looked at her self-image in the tall-looking glass. She had to admit that Colette, the new personal French maid that replaced Healey, was very good. Colette had been trained in Paris and had an amazing talent for hair. Samantha's long thick tresses were swept up in an elegant chignon on the back of her head, and a top knot framed the chignon in an artful twist with light wisps framing her face.

As Samantha studied her reflection, unbidden, an image of Light floated into her mind. As had happened so often in the past week, she pushed the image aside. *Why did he repeatedly cross her thoughts, when she so thoroughly disliked him? Maybe it was because she had never been kissed before, and he had given her*

her first kiss? Or maybe it was because he scared her?

She shivered. As she stared at her image in the looking glass, she remembered those two horrible matrons that had gossiped about her at a soiree one night; they'd wrongly predicted that she'd end up a spinster; she wished she could see their faces now. Once her close friends had left the rural community to enjoy wedded bliss, Samantha had promptly become the fodder for the gossips. She'd tried mightily to ignore the hushed whispers about her floating in muted voices behind fast fluttering fans. Whenever she attended a ball or soiree escorted by her brother Bart, she'd had to blink rapidly to keep the tears at bay, as she'd heard herself being gossiped about.

On one such night at a local ball, while she was hiding from Nathaniel Sweet, she'd overheard two silver-haired matrons discussing her circumstances in detail. She'd been horrified. The ladies were low-level gentry; Mrs. Devonshire, the wife of the town squire, and Mrs. Pigsly, the parson's wife.

"It's such a shame." Mrs. Devonshire had said.

"We all had such high hopes for her."

"But she doesn't have a title, dear. How much hope could one have?" Mrs. Pigsly had retorted archly.

"No, she doesn't—does she—shame. Her father was a commoner, a solicitor, I think." said Devonshire.

"Yes." Mrs. Pigsly had nodded. "He was a commoner." Mrs. Pigsly was rail thin with fine wrinkles crinkling around the corners of her mouth and chin. Loose skin fanned out from under her chin and the skin bobbed every time she turned to talk to her companion.

"I heard he was quite a good solicitor, though."

Pigsly was clearly enjoying the gossip; her watery eyes were bright and rosy as she talked animatedly to her companion.

"She is quite striking, poor lamb," Mrs. Devonshire lamented.

"Surely, she could land someone, perhaps some low-level gentry somewhere, with her looks and her grandmother's connections…"

"Surely, all hope is not lost."

"I hear the grandmother has a title. There is some hope after all, the grandmother is a dowager duchess."

"That is not enough," huffed Pigsly, her neck wobbling vigorously—like a turkey—loose neck skin flapping unbecomingly as she railed on. "Especially if she doesn't have a come-out season in London."

Pigsley whipped out her white fan and spoke in a non-too-hushed voice behind the fan.

"Dearie, no prominent lord is shucking it out here to our sleepy backwater—just for her, if you don't mind me saying."

"Well, they used to," replied Mrs. Devonshire.

"When her mother was alive, they sure did; day and night their carriages pulled in from London. Now that was a lady!"

"True." Nodded Pigsley as she brushed away an imaginary piece of lint from her royal blue evening gown, snapping the fan closed. Both ladies were dressed to perfection in matching royal blue satin gowns.

"Those were the days—but that all ended with her late mother's passing," Devonshire continued.

"You're quite right, though. The mother was a lady! A lady to steal all men's hearts, that one was so gentile' yet so striking. She set the ton on its ear!"

"The daughter doesn't have the mother's vivacious personality, but she has much of her beauty." Mrs. Devonshire reported.

"Why on earth don't they have a come-out season for her? I'm sure she could catch something. Even poor, unfortunate Amy is now a marque's wife, for God's sake."

Even though both ladies were aged, Devonshire had maintained much of her striking looks. She was slim and regal, with thick brown hair lightly streaked with gray and she too had a love for gossip.

"I blame the brother," Pigsly said. "He's now head of the family, and it's quite irresponsible of him to let all her best years fritter away."

"Quite irresponsible. Why Samantha is soon to become an old maid." Devonshire declared.

"I heard that she did get an offer." Pigsley harrumphed. "I heard that kind Nathaniel Sweet made another offer for her—his third—but she turned him down. Again. She's quite uppity, you know? For someone that doesn't have a pot to piss in."

"Or a window to throw it out of!" The ladies said in unison, and then they'd hooted in raucous laughter at their own joke.

"She could do worse than our Nathaniel Sweet," said Pigsley, settling back into the juicy gossip.

On and on, it had gone, and Samantha was quite red-faced by the time she'd heard most of this tirade. Nonetheless, she had held her head up high and returned to the ballroom with as serene an expression as she could muster, all the while wondering how many others in the assembly held similar thoughts. She would show them, she'd vowed. She would make the grandest match of them all. She had resolved to be patient; after all, the parsons did say that good things come to those that wait. And she had waited (throwing in an extra coin to the virgin's statue at every mass for good measure) and it had worked; now her nuptials would be announced in less than a month.

*

She was glad that the next meeting with Light would be on her own home ground. With that bolstering thought, she felt more confident that their next encounter was on her own tuff, especially because her home now looked superb. Feeling more at ease, she spoke to her reflection.

"I'm ready, light, Let the games begin," she purred, and then she quickly left the orangery to go inspect the kitchens.

*

The next evening, after arriving at Evansdale, Light watched Samantha under hooded eyes. His legs were crossed at the ankle as he leaned back in the comfortable settee, looking for all the world to be the picture of refined ennui. His thick black locks catching and holding the reflection of the firelight. His captivating, dark gray eyes were filled with an animalistic desire. Under the guise of boredom, he studied her intently.

The house party was much better attended than he'd hoped. He'd imagined it would be a relatively intimate affair with less than a dozen in attendance. However, over three dozen guests lined the hall, all of them in various stages of glamor, each more dazzling than the next. The attire was much more elaborate than one would expect in the country. Stiff formality hung in the air; it was as if the whole assembly was trying to impress each other with their finery. There was a subtle hostility in their mien, Light wasn't sure of its source.

The young pup had minced no bones about showing his disapproval of Light's suit. Most of the young men in attendance, probably Bart's friends, had sensed the tension and allied themselves with Bart. The old crone sat near the young pup, scowling fiercely in Light's direction as if she wished she could eviscerate him with her gaze.

Lord Light couldn't have cared less about the two of them, and their mutual displeasure with him, his entire focus was on Samantha. She was currently surrounded by five wets behind the ear's swains. The assembly was waiting for dinner to be called. There was an uneven number of men to women, which was odd at a house party. Though, he'd heard some mumbles about a countess that was delayed and would arrive in a few days' time to even the numbers.

Light studied his competition and immediately dismissed them all except for Rigsby. Rigsby's reputation preceded him. Light did not know him personally, but he knew of him. Rigsby was well liked generally by the society matrons, and the gentleman alike. He was a man's man, he participated in every competitive activity available (fisticuffs, horse racing, carriage races) and he usually won. Many chaps usually tossed in their caps in a horse race if Rigsby was competing as he rarely lost. Light moved on from studying Rigsby and scanned the other suitors in the room-dismissing them all instantly. The others were of no importance—young self-absorbed pups without a shred of skill with women. Their only claim to fame was their father's money. He went back to his chief occupation, which was admiring Samantha.

Samantha was impressive in a long golden gown with delicate fichu designs and ivory trim. Her voluptuous breasts discreetly strained the lace and peeked out above the fichu. The translucent skin on her face was slightly tan around her nose as if she'd spent all afternoon sun bathing, which, of course, ladies didn't do in fear of burning their fair skin. It was possible that some expert make-up had created that sun-kissed effect, but nonetheless, he was charmed by it and charmed by her. The overall effect was elegant and stunning.

She did an exceptional job of tolerating the red-headed braying ass that was doing his best to impress her with his wealth. Sir Thomas Edgar Watson, the youngest son of a Baron, who was desperate for her attention and doing his best to keep her attention. Samantha pretended to be interested in what he was saying. Light could tell it was an act because of the tight grip she had on her champagne glass and the fixed smile on her face. She wore a mask of polite interest; he was starting to become familiar with the different masks she wore.

An unwelcome hand suddenly brushed his elbow intimately, and Light turned his hostile eyes to a large-bosomed, red-faced matron with brassy auburn hair. She was studying him intently with her sultry eyes.

Without revealing a sliver of his thoughts, he assessed her, read the offer, evaluated her well-endowed body, briefly considered accepting, then dismissed her. All of this occurred within a few seconds and without a flicker of expression in his handsome features. He decided it was prudent not to accept the matron's generous offer of her body for their mutual pleasure, even though she was beautiful, red-headed, and mature. Until recently, he would have pegged her as hundred percent his type and would right now be charming her out of her camisole. Judging by the length of material stretched across her chest, her breasts would fit nicely in his large hands. But he stood by his decision not to partake of her charms.

He stood and bowed elegantly, kissing her hand elaborately. He wanted to ease his decline of her favors. When in unknown territory, it was best not to alienate anyone, as one never knew who would become useful, when and if an ally was needed. With his body language, he declined politely, and she shrugged as if to say,

"Your loss." *Indeed.*

Chapter Sixteen

Luckily, dinner was announced at just that moment, saving Light the necessity of having to make uncomfortable small talk. The Braying Ass, his new moniker for Sir Thomas Watson, took the liberty of escorting Samantha to dinner and then proceeded to prance around as if he'd scored a big win. Light felt an inexplicable desire to knock Watson on his arise, which was strange because, as a rule, he never allowed himself to rise to the bait of idiots. He followed quietly as the grandmother and Bart (host and hostess) led the way to the dining room, followed by Watson and Samantha, and then the rest of the assembly.

Light was horrified to find the seating arrangements had been assigned in advance by the old crone, their hostess.

"How archaic," he mumbled as he was relegated to the most undesirable seat on the table on the far south end; everyone else of consequence was seated on the north end next to the host and hostess. He sat down stiffly. There was an empty chair beside him on his left and a very fat, unattractive matron on his right, she was a poor relation of one of the guests, she now sieved as a ladies companion.

The matron seemed overwhelmed by him, having never sat near a duke before, she stared silently at her plate for the entire seven courses. On the opposite end of him two elderly spinsters were doing their best to blend into the wall, an occupation they'd likely mastered years ago. The young pup sat at the head of the table with his grandmother on his left and a very beautiful auburn-haired lady on his right. He'd heard her introduced as Serina. Bart was obviously very smitten with the lady as he stared at Serina repeatedly, though discreetly, throughout the entire seven courses. During the meal, the young pup caught Light looking at him and insolently raised his glass in a mock toast in Light's direction. Light caught a look pass between the pup and the old crone. *So, they thought to outmaneuver him, did they?*

One of the goals of this house party was for him and Samantha to get better acquainted in courtship, but with this orchestrated seating arrangement, all he would get to know was an empty chair, his silent dinner companion, and a wallflower or two. Obviously, the family was not as well acquainted with his reputation as they thought. Yes, he was considered the lord of dark; that's why his moniker of Lord Light tickled so many that knew him. But those that knew him very well also knew that he never lost a challenge. Once he troubled himself to partake, he played to win. And for the chance to win Samantha's hand, he more than intended to partake—he intended to win.

Light lifted his glass in acceptance of their challenge. He gifted them with his rare broad grin and then downed his champagne in one swallow. The old crone turned away from him coldly, and he wasn't sure, but he thought he heard her murmur, "Impudent pup."

On hearing that, Light smiled even wider, at last, enjoying himself.

"Let the games begin," he murmured to the empty chair, as he made a one-man toast, clinking his glass himself. The silent matron stared at him questioningly, then resumed staring at her plate.

After everyone had dined and went back to the sitting room, Light wisely studied his competition for the remainder of the evening. The men then retired to the study for a glass of port, leaving the ladies to their tea. While nursing his glass, he digested the rules of engagement given to all the gentlemen while they sipped their port. The house party would last four weeks, with an engagement ball planned at the end. Samantha's betrothal to one of the suitors at this house party would be announced at the final ball to be held at Evansdale in four weeks. Each day, entertainment was planned for all the guests, and competitions were planned for the suitors. Tomorrow there was a hunt planned, and the suitor that bested the others would accompany Miss Samantha to the country dance in three days hence.

The Braying Ass (Sir Thomas Watson), on his third glass of port, was all bravado in his assurances that he would sack the biggest boar in tomorrow's hunt. Light noticed that Rigsby wisely kept silent. But when the men rejoined the ladies, he noticed that Rigsby made a beeline to Samantha's side and stayed possessively close to her for the remainder of the night.

Light assembled all these facts in his head while he carefully studied Samantha under lowered eyes. He undressed her with his eyes under a sultry gaze while appearing to be looking at nothing. She continued to hold his interest, and the veiled hostility around his suit only heightened the challenge, increasing his interest in her. He loved a challenge.

Deciding to send a message to his competitors, who were gathered around her and Rigsby in a swarm, he languidly pushed away from the fireplace. As graceful as a cougar on a hunt, he walked lazily over to her. He caught the uncomfortable looks from her bevy of admirers as they grudgingly made way for his approach. He was a head taller than any of them except Rigsby, and he had a self-possession that none of them could match, so they grudgingly made way. He took advantage of their temporary discomfort and smiled charmingly at Samantha while reaching for her hand. He knew she was too kind to pull away, especially in front of all these people. He had spent enough hours studying her—under a hooded gaze—that he was now able to anticipate her reactions. He'd also observed that she didn't like loud voices. So, he pitched his voice very low but clearly enough to be heard by all her admirers.

"I regret to part with your beauty for even an hour," he murmured in a seductive, entirely improper baritone voice.

It had gotten him into the arms of the town's most beautiful women time and time again. But this time, all his voice earned him from Samantha was a deep frown. Nevertheless, he continued sighing dramatically as if heartbroken.

"But I must retire now if I'm to win the hunt tomorrow."

He looked meaningfully into her hazel eyes, he bent over drawing her hand toward him, and very slowly, almost inappropriately, caressed her wrist with his thumb and then planted a slow kiss on her hand. He felt her pulse jump as his lips contacted a thin vein on her wrist. The sound of her breath catching was music to his ears.

He straightened and looked into her eyes briefly before nodding knowingly to the now stupefied men around her. He felt satisfied that he'd sent his message to them and to Samantha, as well as to the old crone. He was here to win her, and he would not give up easily. And with all eyes on him, he strolled out of the sitting room. A few seconds later, he could be heard whistling a jaunty tune as he climbed the stairs two at a time.

Chapter Seventeen

Light's euphoria lasted all night and into the next morning as his valet dressed him in expensive hunting gear. He wore dark wool trousers cut full through the hips and thighs to allow easy movements. Nestled under his hunting belt was a serrated, double-edged hunting knife with his initials carved into the wood. It had been a gift from his grandfather when he'd been just a boy. He also carried a small horn on his belt along with an ax, coils of rope, and supplies for his derringer. He wore sturdy hunting boots, a loose flowing dark hunting shirt, and his derringer was looped easily over his shoulder by a leather satchel. He looked good and felt even better. It didn't strike him as odd right away when almost no one was awake as he moved around the second floor. He reasoned they were all abed (as aristocrats were inherently lazy), with himself being the exception.

He had woken up early that morning, energized by the upcoming hunt. He was so confident in his hunting skills, and he so eagerly anticipated the crestfallen look on Braying Ass's face when Light landed the largest boar, that his usual attentiveness was dimmed. All these thoughts floated around his brain so jovially that it took him several minutes for his senses to register that something was wrong.

He descended the huge, winding stairs that were decorated with expensive heirlooms along the way. He found the dining room and loaded a big plate of food. He hummed tunelessly around the room while he selected food from the ladder, and then he seated himself. His plate was loaded with braised chicken, sliced ham, a rasher of bacon, fried quail eggs, fresh bread, and black coffee.

The room was empty, but he just assumed he was the first one up. He checked his timepiece again, reassured that he was early by at least thirty minutes. A grizzled butler served him his tea, and he noticed that the entire house was eerily quiet. His senses screamed at him. He looked around, trying to identify the cause for alarm. He'd learned a long time ago to trust his instincts, as his senses were uniquely sensitive. Something was wrong, but he didn't know what.

"How late does everyone sleep?" he asked the stiff butler, faking a laissez-faire attitude that he was far from feeling.

The aged butler looked startled,

"Why everyone is gone, your Grace. The hunt was moved back an hour. The guests have already broken their fast and started the hunt. The ladies went along in carriages to help judge the winner."

To his credit, Light didn't betray a single concern. A small telltale ticking of his jaw was the only indication of his turmoil. He casually ordered a horse brought around, and once the butler left to do his bidding, Light fiercely threw down his napkin. *That old crone was behind this; he was sure of it! She and the young pup!*

They might have won this skirmish, he conceded, but he would win the war.

After what felt like an eternity, the most decrepit, broken-down old horse was brought around to him. The thing looked to be on its last leg.

"What is this!"

Light demanded, his ire finally rising.

The young ostler looked frightened as he studied Light's size and fierce expression.

"It's—it's—it's all that's left your grace," the young boy stammered.

"How about my own horses?" Light said between gritted teeth with a barely restrained temper. He knew it was not the boy's fault.

Light calmed his tone. "I came here on a carriage and brought at least four strong horses."

"Lord Rigby said that since yours were the best horseflesh in the country, he was sure that you wouldn't mind if he transported Lady Samantha in your carriage with the horses. He said he was confident that you would want her to travel in nothing but the best."

Was he to be outmaneuvered at every turn!

Light gritted his teeth. Rigsby, as well as the old crone, was trying to circumvent him.

"I'll give you your just desserts, Rigsby," he vowed.

"Sir?" whispered the young ostler, looking as if he were on the verge of a faint.

"Nothing," Light said calmly, his irritation building.

"Saddle that poor, miserable beast, and let's get this over with," he groused.

As Light vaulted onto the unstable horse, he looked up and saw the old lady hobble to the front of the wide foyer. She'd evidently been listening to the entire exchange between him and the young ostler.

She nodded at him and smiled broadly at the ridiculous look of him on the straggly animal, his long feet almost dragging on the ground. It was clear she was enjoying the sight.

Light nodded at her acknowledging her victory, and then he trotted off as dignified, as he could manage on the bedraggled animal. Behind him, he heard her full hearty laughter.

Chapter Eighteen

Lord Light was sure that he had arrived in an early purgatory. He didn't doubt that purgatory was where he was headed, he was just surprised that he'd arrived there premortem as opposed to postmortem. He sat at the evening's dinner table in his same spot by the empty chair while everyone, including Samantha, was worshiping Rigsby like some living god.

Rigsby had sacked the biggest boar that anyone had seen in recent history. By the time Light's haggard horse had transported him to the hunt site, all the action was over.

Now at dinner, the story of the hunt was retold over and over again in agonizing detail, with Rigsby featured as the conquering hero. Rigsby was soaking it all up like some despot that was owed adoration by all. The old crone had a self-satisfied, jovial look on her face, and the young pup looked at Light first with glee and then disdain. Bart then completely dismissed Light for the remainder of the evening as if he were beneath his notice, a cut direct.

The seating had supposedly been realigned to allow everyone to sit beside someone new, but unfortunately, Light's seat had not been changed, and he still sat in between an empty chair and the fat, silent lady. Even the big-bosomed matron that had offered him her favors the night before now soundly ignored him, her eyes glued on Rigsby.

All this would have been enough to discourage any man and have him packing his bags to London forthwith. As chance would have it, the assembly was not through with Light as yet. To add insult to injury, they constantly bombarded him with insincere apologies about the mix-up over the start time of the hunt.

"Shame, your grace, that you had to miss the hunt," Lord Rigsby said for the third time that night. And each time he did so, a chorus from the other suitors joined in end masse to express their false sympathy.

"Shame," they all said in unison, stretching the vowels in the word as far as they could, sounding just like a choir. As if all that was not enough, they then attempted falsely to try to lift his spirits.

"Lord Light, at least you will be gratified to know that as a result of your generosity, Miss Samantha was transported in style and comfort as you would have wished by your superb horseflesh,"

Rigsby stated in between bites of his boar. As the winner of the hunt, he had been seated beside Samantha, and he reached over and squeezed her hand, running his thumb along her wrist in imitation of Light's brazen caress the night before. Samantha withdrew her hand, her face warm.

A general murmur of "Quite right" was hummed in unison by the choir, following these false declarations.

"So good of you, old man," said Braying Ass to Light.

"What a chap," said another.

"Here! Here!" said another, raising a toast to Light. On and on it went. Samantha didn't join in as all lifted their glasses in a mock toast to Light, a frown creasing her smooth brow. *So, the lady was astute, was she?* She read the undercurrents at this table and knew that despite appearances, all was not well at this table, especially between Lord Light, and Lord Rigsby.

It was a civilized version of watching two fierce bulls

fighting, except the weapons were sarcasm and wit rather than horns and muscle, though the latter was no less intense than the former. Always one to measure his words, Light bit back the retort that sprang to his lips at his opponent's humor at his expense. He had a few choice words in mind for them all, especially Rigsby. However, he found to his surprise that Samantha's obvious distress over the tension at the table concerned him far more than his own current humiliation over this untenable situation. When had a Duke faced such obvious scorn from his lower lords? He didn't know. But more importantly, he realized that he wanted to see Samantha's smiles, not her frowns. In truth, he wanted to see much more of her, but her family's machinations kept him at a far distance at all times. He wanted her, warm and trembling in his arms, open to his every wish. She frowned again, this time worrying her bottom lip incessantly. Light stared at that bottom lip transfixed as she worried it with her teeth. In time the skin on her lips became bruised from the constant friction from her teeth. He stared.

Light stood and toasted Rigsby in a hearty, booming voice, filled with a warm joy de Vivre that he did not feel.

"I should like to make a toast," he said loudly. To Rigsby, a darn good huntsman and an excellent shot."

Here! Here!

Said the choir, lifting their glasses. Light lifted his glass even higher. "May the roof above these friends never fall in, and may the friends beneath this roof never fall out."

Glasses clinked heartily.

"To Rigsby!" was heard from one and all. The mood had significantly lightened.

Lord Light caught Samantha looking at him from across the table, staring at him as if seeing him for the first time. She did not smile, but at least she did not frown. She regarded him with a frank curiosity that gladdened his heart. His eyes drifted to her lips. Alas, thankfully, she had released that full bottom lip from its agitate, and somehow, he couldn't take his eyes away from it. She had been biting it so intensely that she now looked like she had just been kissed within an inch of her life by a not so gentle lover.

Light's blood hummed deliciously in his veins as he continued to stare at her red bottom swollen lips, now red and trembling. In time, she blushed at his too heated, too direct gaze. He looked away, smiling to himself. Yes, he admitted he was in purgatory, but at least with that look and that blush, she had given him a small ewer of water. It was enough. *Enough...for now.*

Chapter Nineteen

Light had been relieved to learn that his bosom childhood companion and cousin, Lord Nicholas Leitchfield Marquis of Devonshire Scotland, had received Light's missive of needing a family member to vouch for him. Nicholas' letter stated he would be joining the house party the next day at Light's invitation.

Light wasted no time informing their hostess. He was buoyed by the news, and in truth, he kept such a small circle of associates and had almost no family to speak of that he'd been at a loss as to who could vouch for him with Samantha's family. His late mother was English by birth, a duke's only daughter, and his late father a noble Highlander from Scotland. Both his parents had died instantly in a carriage accident when he was twelve. Light had no siblings.

After his parents' passing, Light had gone to live with his cousin MacDonald Nicholas and their grandfather, Caelan MacDonald, high up in the Highlands of Scotland. The bond the three men had forged healed a portion of Light's hurting heart over the loss of his parents. He loved Nicholas and his grandfather very much, but when it came time for Light to take up his responsibilities to the dukedom in London, he'd gradually lost contact with both of them.

It was a loss his young heart had never healed from. In time he'd become jaded and cold. Now, as he reflected, he felt saddened by this loss, and he was, in fact, beyond glad that Nicholas had agreed to come and vouch for him, even after all these years.

Nicholas was a charmer and a rake; women loved him and excused him for his outrageous ways because he was boyishly handsome even at five and thirty. The cousins were opposites in every way when it came to looks. Light was muscular, buff, and dark, and Nicholas was gangly, slim, and blonde. Even their temperaments were opposites: Light was somber and brooding, whereas Nicholas was carefree and boyish. Still, the two loved each other dearly. The only feature they shared in common was their eyes, they had the exact same dark gray eyes in shape, coloring, and expression.

Buoyed by the news of Nicholas' coming, Light gathered his valet Simon in his bedchamber for a strategy session late into the night. The men were holed up for the better part of an hour, creating a handmade map of the estate to help them win the next event. Light had ordered his valet to spy for him so that they didn't get outmaneuvered again, as they had on the hunt.

A horse race was planned for the following morning at dawn, and the winning prize was a kiss from Miss Samantha. Light intended to win. The image of her at the dinner table with a swollen red bottom lip had not left him, he wanted to nibble on that lip and nibble on her as well, and he'd make sure that she didn't forget him anytime soon. He intended to win the next game, and he'd be damned if he'd be outsmarted by either Rigsby or the old crone. *Let the fun continue.* He smiled with cockiness as he reviewed the plan again that he and his valet had created. It was perfect; nothing could go wrong.

Chapter Twenty

Light paced up and down for the ninth time that morning. It was race day, and he was an hour early to the race site with his fastest horse, Dionysus. Both Dionysus and his other horse, Demon, were twin thoroughbred horses. He'd had a devil of a time choosing which one to race today. Both were excellent horseflesh, but Dionysus was slightly faster. He had raised both horses from birth and was very much attached to both of them. There were no finer horses in all of London.

He had skipped the morning meal in favor of two honey biscuits that he'd packed hurriedly in his saddlebags, and he now nibbled on one while waiting at the horse site. He hadn't wanted to delay his early arrival at the race site by having a full sit-down meal. He also wanted to savor the look on the faces of Rigby and Braying Ass when they arrived and found him already there. He was determined not to allow this victory to slip away from him like the last one had.

Nicholas had arrived the night before, and it would feel good to have an ally at the dinner table tonight to enjoy his victory with. Nicholas had listened intently to Light's recounting of the disaster in his underground playroom and his thwarted efforts to win Samantha's hand thereafter. Thus far, Nicholas had been both amused and bemused, especially by the hunt debacle. The two cousins had bent their heads together, similar to how they had as children, as they'd studied the hand-drawn map that Light, and Simon had made. The cousins had conspired late into the night and early into the next morning.

When Light arrived at the race site, he was in jolly spirits even though he hadn't gotten much sleep the night prior. He knew that his horse was two hands taller than any other horse in the race. His horse was also twenty stones heavier than any of his opponents' horses. Twenty stones of pure muscle and heart. On top of that, Light himself was an excellent horseman, and he had bonded seamlessly with Dionysys since his birth. The two were so well in sync that when in the saddle, it couldn't be determined where he ended, and his horse began. They flowed together so intimately that they were an extension of one another.

Light again glanced at his timepiece, his glee at the upcoming race giving way to unease. A half-hour remained until they were due to start, and none of the other horsemen had yet appeared. He went over the plan again that he and Nicholas had formulated, looking for flaws. Nothing seemed apparent. He'd covered all the bases.

At last, a horseman appeared. The single rider was riding hell for leather, huge turfs of dirt being kicked up as his horse galloped headlong toward him. The rider was also screaming at the top of his lungs. Light couldn't make out the words, but his sixth sense was ringing. Something was wrong, but he didn't know what. Something about the rider was familiar. Relying on instinct, Light climbed onto his horse and headed toward the rider.

"Lord Light! Lord Light! We're at the wrong place!"

It was Simon, riding Light's other fastest horse, Demon.

Light pulled up beside his valet, not comprehending how this could have happened as they'd gone over the plan repeatedly.

"My Lord!" Simon said, completely out of breath, slowing his horse. "The site of the race was changed late last night. Each nobleman was sent a handwritten note, slid beneath his chamber door. Except us, My Lord! We were the only ones not notified! I found out about the deception a half hour ago after you had already left. I heard two chamber maids laughing about it, and I came straight away."

Light saw red. His fury was truly and earnestly stoked. "Where!" he roared.

"Where have they moved it to?"

"The north side of the property, My Lord. You'll never make it in time. It's twenty clicks away, and the race starts in fifteen minutes. It will take you a half-hour just to get to the starting lineup."

Light quickly turned the reins, looping Dionysys around.

"My Lord! My Lord!"

Simon yelled fruitlessly to Lord Light's retreating back, "You're too late!"

Light was galloping full speed ahead toward the north gate. He urged his horse on faster. From his peripheral vision, he saw Nicholas riding hard to catch up to him. He must have heard of the trickery too and was galloping to support him. Light was in full fury, and he urged his horse on even faster. He didn't recognize himself. He didn't know why all of this should matter to him so much or why he was in such a fury. He tried ineffectually to calm himself while not breaking stride.

Chapter Twenty-One

Twenty minutes later, Light reached the starting lineup. The other riders were just an image of dust on the horizon, so far ahead of him were they. His horse was starting to tire.

"Onward!" he yelled to no one in particular. His horse faltered but again picked up momentum at Light's urging. He had never used a whip. In the Highlands, his grandfather had taught him how to bind with a horse such that no whip was ever needed. He leaned low on Dionysus's back, now, communicating his urgency with every breath. Man and beast struggled together as one.

A few clicks later, Light passed the last rider. He still had a lot more horses to pass before catching the leader, who he recognized as Rigsby.

"Come on, old boy!" Light encouraged his horse.

"You're worth two of any of these nags here."

Light passed another rider and then another. The female spectators waiting at the finish line came into view. Everyone was in their best finery, but only two stood out to Light as he passed the next rider, Samantha and the old crone.

Samantha was genuinely excited to see him, and she clapped her hands as his horse made huge gains toward Rigsby. The old lady, on the other hand, appeared ashen as if seeing a ghost. She was seated regally on an armchair with wheels, fashioned especially for her by a local carpenter. The chair eased the strain on her knees when she had to walk long distances.

A cheer rose up among the guests as Light and Rigsby, the two remaining leaders in the competition, raced like their lives depended on it, toward the finish line, their two superior mounts fighting earnestly for the lead. Rigsby landed a savage blow to his mare with his riding crop, and she surged forward, winning the race by one stride. A loud roar of applause rang out for Rigsby from the entire assembly.

Nicholas had arrived, jumping nimbly off his horse, and he stood stiffly by his mount, watching the riders cheer Rigsby. Light jumped down from his horse and passed long, well-manicured hands up and down his mount's legs and hooves to check for injury.

"You did well, boy." He encouraged Dionysus in a soothing tone, trying to calm the beast, whose heart and lungs were heaving and foam coming from his mouth.

From the corner of his eye, Light watched Rigsby bow to Samantha and soak up the applause as if it was his due. The old crone seemed very discomfited as she announced Rigsby was the winner.

"I hereby declared the Marquis of Devonshire Lord Randall Bradley III our own dear Rigsby as the winner of today's horse race!" she said loudly.

"Could the first and second place winner please approach? The first-place winner will get a kiss from my granddaughter and the second place winner will get a ribbon."

Light approached and stood stiffly next to Rigsby. The tick flickering in Light's jaw was the only outward signal of his inner turmoil. He never knew what possessed him, but something within him rebelled at having to stand there and watch Rigsby kiss Samantha in full view of the assembly. He smoothly sidestepped Rigsby as the old boy was about to make a step forward to kiss Samantha. Light got to Samantha first, and seeing the surprise in her hazel eyes, he tipped her chin forward and planted his full sensuous lips on her lips. Her mouth formed an "O" of surprise, and he used the moment to slide his tongue through and tease her warm lips further apart, but she didn't respond to him.

The assembly was frozen in shock. Just as Light was about to withdraw in defeat, her small, shy tongue met his. He exalted, his energy surging so fast within him that he felt light-headed and unsteady. He pulled her closer and lost himself in her warmth.

"Hey, there I say, unhand her this instant!"

"This is most ungentlemanly!" yelled Rigsby.

Light released a shaken Samantha and bowed elegantly to her and her grandmama. He winked impishly.

"If it's all the same, ma'am," he said to the old crone.

"Rigsby can have the ribbon and the win. I just wanted the kiss."

He clapped Rigsby unnecessarily hard on his back in congratulations and strolled off, leaving a stupefied assembly in his wake.

Chapter Twenty-Two

"Say, cousin," Nicholas easily caught up with Light as he went to retrieve his horse Dionysis. "Since when did you start behaving like a bull in a China shop?" he quipped.

"That was pretty ballsy back there. Don't you think you'll alienate them even further than you already have?"

"Yes, Nicholas, I will certainly alienate them."

Light nodded, staring at the sour looks the old crone and the whole assembly wore collectively except Samantha, who was still fiercely blushing. She delicately declined a kiss from Rigsby, saying one kiss was quite enough for today, as she extended the ribbon. Looking quite put out, Rigsby accepted it and stormed off.

"Alienating them," Light continued.

"Is just not at the top of my list of concerns right now. I almost lamed a bloody good horse because of their deceit! It ends here,

Nicholas!

Now!

They will not find me such an easy target from here on out."

Nicholas grinned broadly.

"Alexander, I'm glad to hear you say that. I thought you might give up. I'm glad you're not packing your bags to go back to London. From the little I've seen of Miss Samantha Minnis; I know, she is worth fighting for."

Light walked easily beside his horse, taking the long way

back to the manor. His horse needed the rest, and he needed to be away from the manor to clear his head.

"Why did you think I would give up?" he queried.

"Wasn't I raised in the Highlands, the same as you?"

Nicholas gave a lopsided grin.

"Yes, cousin, but I barely recognize you any more. You've become such a hoity toity lard. I dinnae think you'd know a fitting spirited lassie when ya set eyes upon her." said Nicholas, easily slipping into a Scottish brogue.

"I was prepared to steal her away from ye." Nicholas continued his teasing.

Light landed a gentle jab to his cousin's ribs, and the two men instantly fell into low crouches in the tall grass, preparing to spar with one another as they had in childhood; they spared all the while laughing like mates. The tension of the last few hours melted away from Light's shoulders as he traded light blows and jabs with his cousin.

*

Light languidly crossed his ankles as he sat sprawled on the settee later that night in the sitting room. His eyes were hooded as he sipped from his own scotch that his own valet had packed for him from Lights' own London cellar. He was glad that his valet understood what "packing essentials" meant. One never knew what swill lurked about in other people's cellars. And a day like the one Light had just endured necessitated a quality Highland scotch from his own secret smuggled stash.

Light surveyed the room. Nicholas was quickly working his charms on the big-bosomed, red-headed matron from a few nights ago, and she was laughing charmingly at his jokes. Light knew what lay in store for those two. Nicholas would likely have her undergarments off before the rest of the assembly had even retired for the night. With steely gray eyes, Light read the still sour looks of the victorious yet soundly defeated Rigsby. The other suitors surrounded Rigsby as they too were joined in their mutual anger against Light. Light couldn't have cared less. He stretched out his long legs languidly, allowing his full six-foot plus frame to lay in repose, ensconced as it were, in the settee, warmed by his scotch. He sipped from his crystal glass leisurely as he waited for Samantha to make her entrance.

Chapter Twenty-Three

As he waited, Light inwardly reviewed his personal plans for winning tomorrow's competition. A boat race was planned. After their friendly sparring yesterday eve the two cousins had bent their heads together and using their best childhood pranks, came up with a plan to win the next series of competitions hands down. *Enough was enough!*

Even now, as the assembly gathered together, Light's valet Simon was loosening the rowlocks on the boat Rigsby would race with tomorrow morning. Light smiled inwardly as he imagined both those oars nicely sliding into the lake. Rigsby would become a sitting duck. A satisfying glee-filled Light's heart. He felt not a morsel of contrition. After all, the bugger had almost caused the laming of a very fine horse. Light fumed every time he thought of it. Besides, it's not as if Light planned to drown the bugger, just slow him down a bit, even though drowning him had briefly crossed his thoughts and then been discarded.

He rose lithely as Samantha entered; he intercepted her hand before the others had noted her presence. He had a sixth sense where she was concerned and that heightened sense always alerted him to her presence. He admired her as he approached, her dinner costume this evening could be considered a bit risqué. It was cut in the latest French fashion, a large expanse of her bare back was exposed, and her creamy skin enticed him. Diamond studding lined the edges of the back hem catching the light and drawing attention to her slim back and rounded derriere.

"Allow me to apologize for my rash and ungentlemanly behavior this afternoon." Light purred as he bent over her hand.

Samantha looked momentarily taken aback; he had moved so quickly toward her from his relaxed pose, she was caught off guard at finding him at her elbow. She quickly recovered, a cool reserve filling her features. Her customary mask slid securely into place, she responded with a cold nod of her head. He felt bereft at losing her true presence while only having a diminished version of her through her cold mask. This frosty hauteur was a new look for her, and Light marveled at it. She would make a fine duchess he inwardly mussed. His duchess that is.

"Think nothing of it," she said dismissively as she started to turn away.

Her cool dismissal sparked something within Light. Intrigue. *When had he ever been so effectively and coldly rebuffed by a female?* Most females of his acquaintance were cloying especially when a duke was in residence. All the while they'd display their various charms to their best advantage to try to get his attention. He pondered this conundrum while continuing to converse with her as if nothing had happened.

"To make amends, he said, please permit me to escort you to dinner," he said loudly to the room at large, purposely needling the angry suitors in the corner, who were just now realizing that she'd arrived.

There was a small, infinitesimal crack in Samantha's hauteur. A spark of unease briefly flickered in her hazel eyes, and then it was quickly gone. Light was afraid that he may have imagined it, but his instincts knew better. *Was she afraid of him?* The thought gave him pause. There was a side of him she hadn't yet seen. He had a kind, caring and humorous side. All she'd seen thus far was, as Nicholas had said, him being a bull in a China shop. He endeavored to become more charming and show Samantha the gentler side of his nature.

While waiting for dinner to be served, he regaled her with amusing stories of himself and Nicholas as they had been as boys. By the time dinner was called, Samantha was struggling to hold back her mirth. While amusing her with his tales, Light simultaneously maneuvered her unobtrusively to the sitting room entrance as they talked, his hand at her elbow (making it impossible for anyone else but him to escort her to the dinner table). He walked easily with her at his side to the dinner table, all the while fielding off dirty looks from her other swains.

He clandestinely signaled to Nicholas, who reluctantly left his big-bosomed redhead and easily loped over to the old crone. In his best courtier's voice that he'd perfected during his service at the French Court, Nicholas begged to be allowed to escort the old lady to dinner.

"There's no need, my Lord. My grandson will do the honors," she said lightly dismissing him with a regal wave of her gnarled fingers.

Nicholas placed a hand over his heart as if devastated.

"Your grandson was just called away, my Lady. It seems an urgent matter needed his attention, but I am at your service. I would be honored if you would allow me to escort you."

He bowed low at her feet and remained prostate there—a supplicant. Everyone paused their conversations to watch the interaction (at once in sympathy with his cause)—a few young ladies even clutching their fans to their bosoms charmed by his constant gallantry.

The old crone looked put out as she stared down at lord Nicholas' prostate form.

"Very well, young man," she said churlishly. If you insist."

"Oh, I do," cooed Nicholas, rising easily.

"I most certainly do," he insisted." He helpfully got onto one side of the lady as her dinner escort.

Lord Light had arranged for Samantha and himself to lead the front of the line, as the assembly headed into supper; especially because, as a reigning Duke, he was the highest-ranking peer at attendance (A fact her family conveniently seemed to forget on a regular basis). As he approached the dining room table with Samantha on his arm, he winked at Esther, the housekeeper. His valet had charmed Ester into re-arranging the seating cards. The old crone and Bart would still be seated at the head of the table as was their right, but tonight, Light would be seated near them at the right-hand side of Samantha, and Rigsby would sit next to the empty chair and the silent matron.

Light gallantly pulled out Samantha's chair. Just as she was about to question the seating arrangements, he launched into another amusing childhood tale. She covered her lips with her hand to keep from laughing uproariously.

"That one reminds me of a similar trick me, Bart and Healey, played on our governess," she said jovially as she sat down.

"Young man, can you pick up the pace?"

He heard the old lady complain from just inside the sitting room.

"One would think you were the one that needed a cane as slow as you're walking."

By the time Nicholas and Samantha's grandmama appeared at the dining table, the first course was well underway.

"What is this?" questioned Samantha's grandmother as she surveyed Light sitting next to her granddaughter. The seating is all wrong."

"Oh dear," a few guests said, laying down their soup spoons

in consternation.

"What are we to do?" asked another.

"We can all go back to our seating from yesterday," grumbled Rigsby, from way down at the south end of the table.

Light continued eating his soup.

"We could," he said mildly.

"But what would be the fun in that?" He winked at the assembly. "I thought the point of re-assigned seats was for all of us to sit next to someone new. I know I'm certainly happy with my new seat."

Samantha blushed as he looked meaningfully in her direction.

The old crone leveled Light with a cold stare. She angrily swatted away Nicholas' hand as he gallantly pulled out her chair and tried to help her sit in her place of honor at the head of the table.

"I can manage on my own very well, thank you."

She said churlishly swatting away his hands. She straightened her spine regally and gracefully sat down. Nicholas located his own seat signaling for the footman to bring him his soup.

A short while later Bart came in apologizing for his lateness. "It was the darndest thing," he said, while the footmen served him.

"Every one of our horses in the barn took off. Me and the ostler had to run them all down and bring them back to the barn."

"What an odd thing," said the countess of Wales, "all of them"

"Most peculiar," said Nicholas.

"But I'm glad you caught them all."

Samantha's grandmother looked from Nicholas to Light and back again.

"Yes," she said coldly.

"Most peculiar."

Chapter Twenty-Four

Light avoided the matron's penetrating stare and became engrossed with his soup, remaining silent for the entire course. The second course commenced. He then focused on being a perfect dinner companion to Samantha. The two kept up a steady stream of conversation throughout the meal, finding an easy camaraderie growing between them. By dinner's end, both were smiling from ear to ear, having thoroughly enjoyed dinner, oblivious to the sour stares from Rigsby and the other suitors seated at the opposite side of the table.

While Samantha turned and answered a question from her brother, Light mockingly raised his champagne glass to Rigsby and the empty chair beside Rigsby. The movement was so quick that only the two men saw it. Rigsby caught the false salute and responded with a frosty stare of his own.

*

Light was finding it more and more difficult to get the Evansdale servants to leak out information for his benefit. They were a tight-lipped group and loyal to a fault. Nicholas and Simon had gotten as far as they could with their charm but couldn't get any further. Even Ester, the housekeeper, refused to talk about her mistress, even though she was obviously in love with Simon. She also declined to re-arrange the seating cards again, despite the fact that Simon cajoled her incessantly and took her on a lover's stroll. The staff was beyond loyal. *Drat!*

Luckily for Light each of the nobles had brought with them; their own servants to ease their travel woes, and those servants were easy game. They were loose-lipped, flirtatious, lazy, and non-stop gossips. Through them, Light's valet learned that another switch was planned for tomorrow's boat race. Both the time and the location would be changed after everyone went to sleep. The new time and place would be slipped under the door of each lord and lady. Light gave up half a case of his best Highland scotch to the servants in exchange for information contained in the letters. But he gave strict instructions that Rigsby must be allowed to come to the boat race at the correct location and on time. He had promised to deliver just desserts to Rigsby, and he intended to do so.

The next morning, while Light was waiting at the dock, he had to admit that his maritime gear looked especially crisp. His valet had outdone himself again. Light wore standard maritime colors sporting the traditional blue and white boating attire. He had loose white trousers with the white loose fitting boating shoes that many nobles in his class preferred when at sea. He had a crisp white ruffled shirt and a cropped blue double breasted blue jacket with silver buttons. His maritime hat was carelessly tucked under one shoulder. The ensemble was comfortable, stylish and allowed easy movement on the rocky boat.

Nicholas was attired in similar colors by his own valet, but he'd opted for a loose-fitting button-up sweater. Nicholas was the lookout for today's escapade. At daybreak, he was on horseback, perched discreetly high up on the tallest hill of the Estate. He could see all the movements of everyone below. If any trickery was afoot Nicholas would ride down quickly from his lookout point and put their backup plan into play. He was stationed midway between the two possible locations of the boat race in case the information the servants had provided was intentionally false. Nicholas used his spyglass to track the assembly as they left Evansdale, and he would communicate his findings to Light by a single bird call.

*

Light stood by the docks, his boat at the ready. A sharp clear bird call trilled in the air a few minutes later. He relaxed considerably and lit a cigar, understanding the signal to mean that all was well. He inhaled deeply of his fine cigar and thought about how fantastic a day this was. He couldn't remember when he'd enjoyed himself more. In this fight with Rigsby over Samantha's courtship, a mischievous childlike spirit had overcome him, lifting some of the oppressive darkness that had swamped him since becoming an orphan. He couldn't remember a time when he'd gone to such lengths to win a woman's hand. He was surprised to realize that he was having fun, especially because Nicholas was in it with him. He had forgotten what a good brotherhood they shared. He vowed never to let their bond slip again.

At short length, he heard the galloping of horses approaching two hours earlier than the time they'd given him last night at dinner. He was joyously anticipating seeing the looks on their faces. He emerged from his perch, where he'd been casually smoking, his cigar billowing fragrant smoke all around him.

"Say!" he cheerily said to the assembly as many stared at him dumbfounded. Samantha was the only one that looked happy to see him.

"What kept you all?" he drawled.

"I thought for sure you all were in for a late slumber." The stupefied assembly looked questionably at him as he rushed to help the ladies down from their horses.

"I've taken the liberty to bring your boat closer to the dock, Ma'am," he said to Samantha's grandmother. "This way, it won't be such a long walk for you."

Samantha smiled gratefully at him while her grandmother harrumphed and grudgingly accepted his hand as he lowered her from her horse. Rigsby's obvious shock at seeing Light had given way to anger; he huffed off, not bothering to help the other ladies dismount. Rigsby marched to his impressive boat on the dock, stopping to hiss vehemently at Light.

"Miss Samantha has already agreed to ride with me for today's boat race," he whispered fiercely to Light.

"Of course," replied Light off-handedly.

"I wouldn't have it any other way. Since everyone else is paired off, I'll just ride alone," he announced cheerily.

Light whistled a merry tune while he walked along the dock to his boat, he hopped in easily with great balance. He then grabbed his oars and waited patiently for the signal to start the race. A large, well-stocked picnic basket lay in the center of his boat, along with a bottle of wine, blankets, and pillows.

Bart rode with his grandmother, while Samantha rode with Rigsby. Nicholas had ridden in a bit late and got into a boat with his busty redhead. The other suitors paired up with other female guests, and everyone waited for Bart to start the boat race.

Bart stood easily on his boat and went over the rules' outlining the path along the river they would race on. Light already knew the path; he had studied it the night before on their hand-drawn map. He looked over at Nicholas; the two cousins communicated to each other silently with their eyes. Light nodded to Nicholas, and when Bart shot the derringer into the air to signal the start of the race, Light leveled his oars in the water and started off purposely, allowing Rigsby and Samantha to take the lead. Nicholas also hung back, staying around fourth place.

About thirty minutes into the boat race, Rigsby swore loudly. "Blast it all!"

Light was the closest to them.

"What has gone amiss, old man?" he inquired loudly while positioning his boat close to theirs.

Bart immediately called a halt to the race. He was not close to the lead, so he was far off. He started to turn his boat around to investigate Rigsby's issue, but Light was there first.

"Our oars lamented, Samantha. They must have sunk into the lake as the ring hook loosened. Shame! Let's give you a hand," Light said.

He reached in, nimbly lifted Samantha out of Rigsby's boat, gently pulled her into his arms, carefully settled her in his vessel, placed a warm blanket around her waist and pillows at her feet and sailed off. All in a matter of seconds.

"Wait!" Rigsby yelled.

"What about me? I just can't stay here!" He bellowed to Light's retreating back.

"Wait!"

Bart had managed to turn around by then. He looked in consternation at Rigsby's stalled boat and looked over at Samantha, sitting comfortably in Light's boat floating away. Satisfied that Samantha was safe, Bart signaled to one of the servants that carried the refreshments to go back and get oars for Lord Rigsby.

"Rigsby, when the footmen come in with your oars, you'll have to let them tug you in. I don't want you to risk rowing until we get that rook hook fixed, Bart instructed. All right, everyone," Bart yelled.

"We must continue. We don't want the ladies to get too much sun."

The other suitors mumbled their apologies to Rigsby as they rowed past him.

"Shame about your oars, Rigsby." said one.

"Sorry about that, old man," said another.

"They'll have you out in a jiffy," said Braying Ass.

"Yes, Rigsby!"

Light shouted from the lead.

"That's such a shame. Oh well," he shrugged.

"Keep your head up, old chap, and try not to get too much sun."

"Quite right!" Joined in Nicholas, rowing past Rigsby and moving into the second-place spot, with his buxom redhead floating by his side sipping lemonade.

Samantha's grandmother stared coldly at Light as he sailed past them with Samantha in tow. He stood briefly on the bow of his boat and bowed respectfully to her. He then seated himself and rowed vigorously. She harrumphed. Samantha stared directly at Light, her knowing hazel eyes assessing him silently. He smiled sheepishly and shrugged. He couldn't take his eyes off her as she reclined in elegant repose on the pillows, his cashmere blanket wrapped around her hips. Space seemed to open up, and time slowed as they stared at each other, a push-pull energy igniting instantly between them. Words became unnecessary as they floated on the calm water in harmony.

Light expertly maneuvered the boat past all the other boaters. But Nicholas proved to be much less of an expert boatsman. He constantly got in everyone's way, and then it took him forever to extract himself. But he seemed to have an endless supply of lemonade, fruit, cheese, and every delicacy imaginable to keep his buxom maritime companion happy. Everyone had to wait while he tried to extract himself from their path, and while he poured her more lemonade and then one for himself.

"Lord Nicholas, do hurry up!" berated Samantha's grandmother at her wits end with his antics. His boat was blocking everyone's path again. He seemed to know where all the narrow paths were in the vast river. He invariably got there first but then got stuck time and time again.

"My apologies, Ma'am. I'm all thumbs on these contraptions. Would you like some lemonade?" Nicholas offered charmingly.

With all the mayhem Nicholas was causing, Light got so far ahead from the assembly that he couldn't even see the other boaters any more. When he had reached at least a twenty-minute lead, he rowed his boat under a bridge, secured the oars, and opened the over-large picnic basket at his feet. He handed Samantha two oranges, a large hunk of cheese, fresh bread, grapes, cold pheasant, and a glass jar filled with cold lemonade.

"A feast," she said, amazed. "When did you have time to pack all of this?" she inquired, munching on a bit of delicious cheese and grapes. Samantha was finding it hard to take her eyes off of him. His strong dark physique blocked off the sun as he worked. He gingerly laid a blanket over the picnic basket, pulling out a plate covered with fresh honey biscuits and putting it on top of the blanket (covering each biscuit with clotted cream and melted blackberries). A frown creased his brow as he worked. He was being as attentive to his task as if it were the piece de la resistance in his obvious seduction scheme. She was charmed despite herself. Never had she pictured Light as a romantic. But of late, he was pulling out all the stops. Up to now she had pretended to be ignorant of all the underhanded tricks she'd seen her family and Rigsby playing on him. But she had to admit that he'd held up rather well under pressure. She was now conflicted about his suit. Her kind nature always cheered for the underdog. But which was he was he the underdog? Or a wolf in sheep's clothing?

After feeding her a sweetened honey biscuit dripping with clotted cream; he peeled her a fragrant orange and then fed her small bits of orange. He then joined her on the pillows, laying his long frame in repose beside her. "When did I have time to plan all this?' he replied to her earlier question." "I have my moments," he murmured, transfixed as he watched the sweet orange nectar dribble down her chin. Her tongue darted out to capture its juice, Light groaned with frustration. She looked disapprovingly at him. He shrugged sheepishly. They leisurely enjoyed their impromptu picnic and shared some wine. He licked the remains of the pheasant off from her fingers, pulling each digit seductively in his warm mouth. The shade of the bridge and the cool sounds of the lake lulled them into relaxation.

Chapter Twenty-Five

At length, Lord Light's sensitive ears heard the approach of the other rowers. He pulled everything back into his basket and recaptured the oars, while Samantha drew on her gloves and arranged her parasol.

"What exactly are you doing under that bridge, Light?" her grandmother inquired as soon as she came around the bend, fury and suspicion etched on her face.

"Me?" he asked innocently.

"Just resting a spell."

The race resumed, and by its end, Light had managed to take Samantha to three secluded places on the river while they waited for everyone else to catch up; the others were constantly blocked off by an inept Nicholas, who struggled to get his boat out of their way. The last spot that Light took her to was one of Samantha's favorite spots on the estate, and she marveled that he had found it.

It was a small secluded waterfall where the path appeared closed off but then suddenly opened to a peaceful scene where water tumbled down the large rocks. Samantha fondly remembered that she, Bart, and Healey had played in it for countless hours as children.

It was here that Light finally claimed a kiss. Samantha was surprised that she went into his arms so easily. Her curiosity had been building up during the long boat ride, and she allowed herself to experience what a mutual kiss felt like. Before now, each time he'd dominated her and taken the kiss. She wanted to feel what it was like to share a kiss. She'd waited so many years for her first real kiss; and now curiosity drove her, along with her own inquisitive nature. She shyly dove her hands into Light's silky, thick locks. She'd imagined what they'd feel like, and she hadn't been wrong; they were as soft and silky as they looked. His sandalwood scent, the humming of the waterfall, the warm sun and the heated look in his eyes all effectively seduced her, she sighed going into his arms easily.

"Alexander," she murmured, sliding her fingers into the silky hairs at his nape. She'd said his name. Intense pleasure tore through him from the throaty sound of his name on those lips. He lowered his lips over hers lost. It didn't occur to him to mind that she'd used his Christian name without asking permission. They were equals; he now accepted that fact unequivocally.

Light stilled as her fingers grazed his scalp, and he groaned deep in his throat at the contact. He crushed her to him, pressing her deeper into the pillows—while sipping the nectar from her lips. She tasted like lemonade and something else; a sweet taste- all of her own. He drew her full curvaceous body deeper under him, the swaying of the boat rocking them both in a sweet rhythm. He continued to feast on her lower lip, enticing her tongue to mate with his. He forgot she was a maiden, devouring her lips hungrily. She clutched him tightly in response, roaming her fingers freely over his midnight locks. He felt like he was drowning. At length, he released her upon hearing the noise of the approaching boaters.

He eased them both back into the path of the others, and minutes later, the other boaters joined them. His breathing was ragged, and his hair was badly disheveled. When Samantha's grandmother scowled at him, for once he looked contrite and bowed his head looking away.

Later that evening, Light and Samantha were announced as the first-place winners of the boat race. A red-faced burnt Rigsby stood stiffly among the guests offering his congratulations.

"Sorry, you had to miss it, Rigsby."

Light said jovially and slapped Rigsby light-heartedly on the back, a bit heartier of a slap than was strictly needed. Rigsby winced involuntarily from the brash contact with his sunburnt skin.

Rigsby took an involuntary step forward as Light shook his hand forcefully.

"There's always next time, hey?" chimed in Nicholas, who also playfully slapped Rigsby on the back. Another mighty slap that launched Rigsby another step forward.

As the winner of the boat race Light was allowed to escort Samantha to the Huntington Ball at the neighboring estate planned for two days hence. The way she'd looked invitingly at him in the boat this afternoon had not left him, he eagerly awaited a chance to hold her in his arms again in a waltz. Strictly speaking since she had never had a come out, she wasn't allowed to Waltz, Light puzzled over the dilemma intent on solving it.

"My Lady," Nicholas asked Grandmama.

"I am the only gentleman at this event that has yet to be allowed to escort Miss Samantha and enjoy the pleasure of her company at dinner. May I do so tonight?"

Nicholas asked humbly in his best courtier's voice, speaking loud enough for all to hear as he bowed low.

"If perhaps," he clutched his chest dramatically.

"I can be so lucky."

Whereas Light kept a somber distance from the guests, Nicholas was the life of the party. Somehow, his charm always earned him easy forgiveness from the ladies. Nicholas never sat near his cousin, presenting himself as a neutral party. He had, one by one, charmed all the ladies present. Grandmama scowled at him now, but she was just as captivated by his antics as everyone else.

"I suppose so," she said cautiously.

"You can escort Samantha to dinner tonight and sit beside her at the meal. I don't see any harm in that."

Nicholas bowed low in thanks and proceeded to flatter her incessantly until dinner was called.

"May I compliment your hair, my Lady? It's so regal, and your gown is so elegant. Is it French? May I also compliment you on your taste in your costume tonight…"

He rattled on and on.

By the time dinner was served, Grandmama looked quite harassed, and she was glad to be rid of Nicholas and his constant flattery.

At dinner after the footmen had cleared away the third course, Light spoke up from his exiled position at the base of the table near the empty chair, where he had once again been relegated by the host and hostess.

"Is anyone else feeling a draft here?" he inquired blandly. "It's quite drafty."

Everyone looked up in dismay.

"No, my Lord," said Isabella Baroness of Wales.

"Me neither," Contessa replied to the lady's companion. "Not I," another guest stated.

"I don't feel a draft," said Braying Ass.

"But perhaps it is coming from the windows near your seat, he suggested helpfully."

"Say, cousin," Nicholas said gallantly.

"Why don't you take my seat?" He then held up a note a footman had just given him.

I have just been informed of a pressing matter at one of my Estates. I have to attend to it forthwith. I'll have to excuse myself—pardon me he said to Samantha and her grandmother. Alexander, he said to his cousin, "Since there's a draft down there, here-take my seat."

"Well, if you insist." Light stood up immediately, straightening his flawless cravat.

"If you're sure, Nicholas?" he asked, already moving fast to take his cousin's seat. The footmen rushed to reseat Light and transfer his plate to Nicholas' seat as Nicholas speedily vacated it to attend to his pressing "business."

"That's much better," Light said to the assembly at large as he sat down next to Samantha.

"It was quite drafty down there," he said innocently looking plaintively at Samantha's Grand'Mere.

She looked at him dumbfounded, and then she turned her attention away, smiling brightly at the guest on her right, ignoring Light.

Light smiled warmly at Samantha, as he made himself comfortable at her side. He nodded coldly at Rigsby, who sat on her left-hand side. The meal resumed with everyone content except Rigsby and the old lady,

Chapter Twenty-Six

Alexander Litchfield, Lord "Light" (Duke of Ennsbury), was in high spirits. He and Nicholas were steadily maneuvering things to his favor. Either by wit, brawn, or trickery, he was declared the winner and champion of each competition. And most importantly, with Nicholas's help, Light always managed to sit close to Samantha at supper. His suit was at last progressing well. Samantha was wearing her aloof detached mask less and less. Every time she ran her clear hazel eyes over him, he felt more and more connected to her. It warmed his cold soul, filling him with patience and joy.

Nicholas, as the golden-haired neutral boy, had far more access to Samantha than Light did. Nicholas took her and the other ladies on carriage rides, picnics and strolls. And low-and-behold, Light always made an unexpected appearance. Invariably Nicholas would be called away by his valet on some urgent matter, and his cousin Alexander would step in gallantly to fill in for him and accompany Samantha in Nicholas' stead.

All was going well. After all, all was fair in love and war. The only thing that marred his good humor was the appearance of Countess Patricia Lowell one warm afternoon. He was shocked to discover that the long-awaited countess that was supposed to even the odd numbers for the house party—was his disgruntled former lover and mistress.

"Hello, Light," she said coldly, looking from him to Samantha at their joined hands and matching smiles. "Fancy seeing you here." she purred. "I see you have been busy." She indicated to Samantha's hand in his as he and Samantha had just returned from a lovers stroll in the garden, the two were all smiles, and laughter.

He'd been pleased to discover that as a recent novice to kissing; Samantha was eager to make up for lost time. As often as not, she pulled his black head down to her lips whenever they were alone, sinking her fingers into his dense, thick locks to lock him into place. He began to suspect that under her cool, aloof mask, she hid a very passionate nature.

He was wearing a broad ,happy grin split from ear to ear until he heard Patricia's familiar voice. He hid his shock at seeing Patricia by executing a low bow over her hand-his mind racing in panic.

"Patricia," he said coldly, kissing her hand, the icy fingers of dread reaching up to clutch his chest as he straightened.

Since ending their affair last year, Patricia had become a starch enemy—a woman scorned, as the Bard had so aptly described. Especially fitting was the quote, "Hell, hath no fury as a woman scorned." The Bard must have known Patricia personally.

Dread filled his belly as Patricia stared at his joined hands and Samantha (her lips were red and swollen, and her cheeks were rosy). His courtship with Samantha had been going so well. This had to be the work of the old crone! *Checkmate.*

"Come, my dear," Patricia said languidly to Samantha, peeling Samantha's hand from Light's tight grip. "Let's have some girl talk, shall we? Off you go, Light." She'd fluttered her glove at him, effectively dismissing him.

He walked off on leaden feet, an inner scream filling his head. *No!!!!! He thought wordlessly as he moved away.*

*

Samantha had returned from her walk with Patricia an hour later, ashen-faced. She'd refused to make eye contact with Light, and rather, she'd gone straight to her rooms, skipping dinner that night.

For the next three days, she refused to come out of her rooms. Every night, she'd sent a note to the assembly apologizing for missing the evening meal, claiming a migraine.

Light now longed for the empty seat once he realized it had been held vacant for Patricia. She smiled knowingly at him during the meal, enjoying his misery.

"It's a pity Samantha has to miss dinner again tonight?" she purred at him. "I hear she has a delicate constitution. I wonder what could have upset her?" She batted long silky eyelashes at him, clearly enjoying herself.

"Excuse me," he said to all the ladies, laying down his napkin. "I've suddenly lost my appetite." He stood and left.

"Shame," he heard Patricia murmur to his departing back. "More wine, anyone"? she asked innocently.

He retreated to his rooms to pace, and a few hours later, Light was still pacing. He was beside himself. He wanted nothing short of climbing the trellis to Samantha's rooms and demanding to know what lies Patricia had fed her. He'd never felt so miserable in all of his life. Defeat set in. He'd tried his best to court her, but he'd lost; he felt so bereft.

*

As luck would have it, Light's grandfather made an unannounced visit to the Evansdale house party the following morning. This news had initially been a shock to everyone, but as Light spent time in the old man's grounding presence that next morning, he felt their connection returning, and a sense of calm filled him. The men had a genuine love for one another, and they also had an uncanny resemblance to each other. Light felt as if he was looking at an older, more sober version of himself. His grandfather stood tall and erect, still muscular and brawny, with a tan leathery face that had weathered many seasons. His steely gray eyes looked across the assembly, shrewdly assessing it. In milli-seconds, he knew who had substance and who was all chaff. The proud highlander had aged well; only the streaks of gray in his black hair marked his true age.

With Samantha's absence, (as she stalwartly remained in her rooms), the vitality seemed to have ebbed away from the house party. The men sat in small clumps and brooded, and the ladies flitted about aimlessly. It had been with no small measure of relief when his grandfather had clapped him hardily on his back later that morning. His grandfather had looked meaningfully at the tense Sassenach faces at the manor.

"Let's blow off this place for a time." He said. "I want to share a drink with my two grandsons in peace for a few hours."

*

Samantha was visibly shaking. Every time she replayed the conversation in her mind between herself and the countess, she paled. Patricia's tears had freely flown down her perfect face as she'd recounted her folly at being Light's paramour.

"He is an animal, Mon Cherie. A man sans honor. He beat me viciously for his own pleasure. You're an innocent girl, and while I cannot tell you more, I did want to warn you. A woman is a man's property. Yes? I got away from him because I did not wear his ring, but if you become his wife, you will belong to him, Mon Cheri. There will be no escape, and if he wills to beat you, you won't be able to escape him, n'est pas. By law, you will be his property. It is folly or, as you British say, foolhardy, no?"

Something about the countess's voice didn't quite ring true. But Samantha had seen that awful room with her own eyes. Anyone that had a room like that in their home was capable of anything. But she had also caught a kinder glimpse of him the last few days, a gentle side, though it could be a front. But a part of her heart ached for him once she'd glimpsed that other side to him; because of his gentleness and caring.

But what if Patricia was right? She thought as she paced around her rooms. She'd be trapped in a violent marriage with a man who beat her for his own pleasure. Fear gripped her, and she couldn't breathe. She had to get some air. The mountains by the lake, she always felt peaceful there. It was early morning. If she left now, she'd be back by dinner time.

*

Later that night, Light, Nicholas, and their grandfather were seated at a local pub enjoying a good lunch of kippers, veal, and ale and laughing hard about old times. Light spent all afternoon just enjoying being with his family. As he'd gotten more and more jaded in London, he'd forgotten how good it felt just to be with family. The acceptance, the camaraderie, the good-natured jabs, and most of all, the love and support. Even though he'd all but forgotten them, Nicholas and his grandfather were here to support him now. He was fighting for his future with a woman he cared for very much, and it felt good not to be in the fight alone. He vowed not to let his family slip away again. Hours passed, and the men ordered more food. They stayed another hour after dinner for one last drink, neither ready to return to Evansdale Manor.

Alexander! Help me. I'm so cold. The lake is freezing

Lord Light slowly looked around, the color draining from his face, he'd heard Samantha's voice…something was wrong. His senses were buzzing. He felt cold, and he could feel danger, but he was unsure what was the cause of these feelings. His sixth sense continued buzzing, and he stood suddenly feeling light-headed.

His grandfather gave him a curious look and then stood as well, leaning in close to him so they couldn't be overheard. "What is it?" he asked in a low tone.

Light shook his head. "I don't know," he said dizzily. "I get the feeling that Samantha is in trouble, but I don't know how I know that, but I know."

His grandfather studied Light's face intently as if looking for something, and then he nodded decisively. "Tell me everything," he said.

Light hesitated, sitting down and looking quizzically at both men, as what he was about to say sounded bizarre, even to him, but as he looked at MacDonald's calm face, he felt reassured. MacDonald sat down and waited patiently. At length, Light said in low tones, "I think Samantha is in trouble he said to both men. I don't know how, but I heard her whispering something, and I felt…" he stopped, confused.

"Go on, Lad," his grandfather said, staring at Light intently. "What did you feel?" Light ran a frustrated hand through his hair then continued.

I felt icy cold for a split second, and then I felt shock. I think she's scared. I heard her say, *'Alexander, help me. I'm so cold. The lake is freezing.'* I heard it as clear as day, as clear as I'm hearing you right now.

After listening intently, his grandfather sprang into action and began issuing orders. He turned to Nicholas.

"Nicholas, go back to Evansdale Manor and check on the welfare of Miss Samantha. If she is there, do not leave her side. Be her personal guard. If she is not there, investigate her whereabouts and send a missive back here to the pub with details. His valet will know what to do if he gets your missive. Alexander and I will check the main roads for overturned carriages."

In minutes, the three men parted to carry out their various orders. Light was lost in thought. *Had he really heard Samantha's voice, and how was such a thing possible?* A sense of unease gripped his stomach. Something was not right; of that he was sure. He knew he wasn't completely sure about everything, but somehow, his senses were telling him something, and he had to trust himself for Samantha's sake.

His grandfather gripped his shoulders and solemnly said, "Lad, look at me. It's never happened to me personally, but in the Highlands, we have a legend of a fated couple that loved each other so intently that their souls merged. They were actually able to hear each other's thoughts but only when one of them was in grave danger or extremely agitated."

Light felt like his mind was split in two. On the one hand, hearing this legend relieved him, but on the other, he began to worry that he was going mad. Did this mean that Samantha loved him and that he loved her? It would explain why he had been acting so out of character since he met her. Normally he'd be struggling to remember her name by now, but instead, he was in a frenzy to find her, and at that moment, nothing would give him greater pleasure than to see her beloved face again.

Light and his grandfather traveled the main road for over an hour. At first, he hadn't been too sure which way to go, but as they rode on, he felt very confident they needed to get off the main road and head toward the lake.

He slowed his horse and then stopped. His grandfather looked at him questioningly but didn't speak. He was a man of very few words. The silence lengthened, he looked toward the loch, and his grandfather followed. Light led them off the road for another hour, and they came to a fork in the path. Light hesitated briefly and then went right, his instincts guiding him. The fog ahead crept in as they rode on, and the night sky was darkening.

Another fork came up. "Which way?" his grandfather inquired.

Light shook his head. "Hell, if I know. This whole thing is crazy."

"Stop talking like a Sassenach and listen to your intuition as I taught ya," his grandfather said.

Light looked at the road and shook his head, his frustration evident. "I don't know!"

"Quiet your mind." His grandfather said languidly as if they were on a casual outing and discussing the weather.

Light felt his ire building. *How could the old man be so nonchalant?*

Then he felt it, a very slight nudging.

That way.

"That way!" he shouted and urged his horse onto the trail.

He led them sharply up a side of a mountain; it was a very treacherous trail with a wide, deep loch surrounding the base of the mountain. As they followed the trail, the men heard the wails of a dying animal. They were completely surrounded by fog and darkness now, and their mounts were spooked by the sounds.

They got down and guided their animals by hand, speaking to them in Gaelic. Moving as one, they found an overturned carriage up ahead. It had been pulled by one horse, and the mare was trapped underneath the carriage, its leg broken. Her wails had subsided to painful moans, and there was no telling how long the mare had been trapped under the carriage.

Light's grandfather led his horse gracefully near the animal and tied him to a nearby tree. In Gaelic, he spoke soothingly to the scared, injured mare as he inspected her leg.

"She can't be saved," he announced. He said an ancient prayer in Gaelic and leaned his forehead to the mare's forelock reciting a litany of words. He then leaned back on his heels with one motion unhooking his scabbard. He lifted his knife high in the air and brought it down swiftly over the mare's heart, finding his mark even in the darkness. She shuddered and then lay still. He then gently shut her eyes and wailed a low guttural sound in his baritone voice, rising and falling rhythmically like a headnote. Silently, the majestic moment overwhelmed both men.

Unconsciously, Light had dropped to his knees. At length, they both rose and inspected the overturned carriage. Light quickly built a fire for some light, and he was then able to make out the Evansdale Manor crest. They found the body of the driver and one golden slipper.

"Samantha's," Light said definitively. "And she's nowhere to be found." He studied the scene before him intently and dissected the events that occurred, his intuition guiding him. A picture of what happened formed in his mind, and he spoke. "The horse got spooked, probably from the fast-approaching fog; the horse charged up the mountain," he said, pointing at the tracks. The driver lost control, and he must've gotten thrown here, he said, pointing at a deep imprint in the ground, and when the horse stopped abruptly here, he pointed again at a higher imprint in the ground. Then she was also thrown; she must be in the loch."

The enormity of the hopelessness of her plight dawned on both men. The loch was a vast icy cold tundra lined with jagged rocks upon rocks, and they were currently suspended some sixty thousand hands above the water's edge with no moonlight to guide them. And with the thick fog that had set in hours ago, there was no way to know where to begin the search for Samantha. They would need a search party the size of an army to scour the entire loch. One thing was clear, if Samantha was alive, and that was a big if, she couldn't survive long out there.

Despair filled Light's heart, but he brushed it aside and walked back to his horse, Demon. Demon was Samantha's best chance at survival; he was as sure footed and intelligent as any bloodhound. Light brought Samantha's slipper up to the horse's nostrils and talked to him in Gaelic. Then, once man and beast understood each other, he climbed up on his horse.

"Where are you going, man?" His grandfather blocked his path. "You can't save her, Alexander. The fog is too thick. It's suicide. You'll both die."

"Then I'll die," Light said flatly as the two men stared each other down, neither giving quarter.

"Bloody hell! Wait up then," Caelin said, conceding to Light's wishes. He was not ready to sacrifice the life of his grandson.

"No," Light said, unwilling to risk the old man's life. He'd already lost too many people he cared about and now possibly Samantha. "There are some things a man must do himself, and this is one of them for me. This one is mine, it's my woman, and my fight, but I am beyond grateful that you are willing to stand with me in this. Stay here, he ordered, and pray to whoever the hell you were just talking to back there and if I don't come back, know this, old man; I love you. I always have, and I always will." And with those few words, Light turned his mount down the trail and was gone.

Chapter Twenty-Seven

Light carefully climbed down the steep mountain to the base of the loch, he waded into the icy water with his horse as far as Demon could go. But he wouldn't forfeit his horse's life. Demon deserved better than to be buried alive in this cold watery grave. Light knew that Demon would at least point him in the right direction so he allowed that, but he planned to release Demon before it was too late.

Demon swam in the inky, black waters of the loch, the icy cold water making both their limbs go numb instantly. At length, Light ordered his horse to go back to shore, but Demon neighed, refusing. Light uncharacteristically slapped his horse's rump, but he got a nasty glare in return. He forcibly sent his horse back to shore and swam onward on his own to find Samantha. Resigned Demon turned away and headed back to shore. Light kicked strongly to get his blood flowing and to keep his body from going into shock. Fog surrounded the murky water, and with no moonlight, Light couldn't see anything, but he knew Samantha was in there (somewhere) he sensed her presence. He could feel her panic, and it filled him with dread. *What if he was too late?* The thought caused him to lose focus as he swam in circles. He dove down into the inky depths and lost his way on the swim up. He started to panic as his shirt was hooked by a rock that wouldn't let go. He pulled savagely, and his pants were torn as he came up from the depths gasping for air. He jerked his head above the water and took a big gulping breath, ripping the cloth free as it again got caught on another rock. He knew he was Samantha's only chance for survival, so he never gave up, diving in again and again looking for her.

He looked around hopelessly; he could see nothing, and he was freezing. If Samantha had even survived the fall, which was a big if, she could never have survived this devastating cold darkness. The water froze a man's nuts down to his soul.

"I don't think I believe in you any more!" he shouted to the sky above him. "I haven't believed in you since you took both my parents away from me and left me an orphan!" Tears he'd held back since age twelve flowed down his face freely. "But I need you now! I need you now! If you exist, help me." he groaned. He listened with his whole body for a shred of sound, but the numbing cold was dragging his body down.

Nothing.

"Damn it! Why do I still pray to you!" he shouted to the empty sky. "Either there is no God, or you don't care. You never have."

Light dove back down into the inky blackness, refusing to give up. The futility of his mission weighed down on his soul. Again and again, he swam in random directions.

This way.

He felt the words inside his head rather than hearing them. He turned in the direction of the words. Then he saw it. A scrap of gold-yellow cloth caught his eye. It was snagged on a jagged rock. The rock was sticking up in the middle of the loch like frozen fingers. It kept his attention as he swam toward it carefully, avoiding the sharp edges. A few more strokes of swimming in that direction, and he saw her.

It was Samantha.

The water burned his lungs as he swam faster, but he didn't

care; he had to get to her. She lay so still in the water. Somehow, she had missed landing on the rocks. Her dress had caught onto the edge of the rock and billowed out around her, creating a floatation device of sorts. Her feet were bare, and she was so still that she looked like a broken doll. The faintest of moonlight broke through the fog, allowing Light to find his footing on the sharp rocks and rip through the fabric that kept her buoyed. He saw a large bruise where her head had been bashed by a rock, blood flowed freely, but he didn't see any other trauma. However, she was unconscious. *Was she dead?* Without realizing it, tears sprang to his eyes. *She looked so pale!*

Unable to free her dress from the rocks, he unbuttoned all her stays, grateful for the slight moonlight. He ripped a long length of fabric from her dress and tied it around her head. Once she was in her bare shift, he knotted off the makeshift bandage. He then pulled her against him and started to swim back the way he'd come.

As he whistled for Demon, he felt his legs start to give out from the mind-numbing cold. If he didn't get out of these elements soon, his rescue would have been for naught. He and Samantha would be found frozen to death the next day. Without knowing what prompted it, as he swam, he pressed cold lips to Samantha's lips. Perhaps it had been an unconscious goodbye.

But then, her tongue peeked out between frozen lips and tasted his. So shocked was he that he almost dropped her.

She was alive!

And she was kissing him back.

He didn't know which astounded him more—that Samantha was alive or that she kissed him back.

Light began to kick harder. *She was alive! His Samantha was alive!* He was finding it hard to contain his emotions. She had stolen his heart with her beauty and innocence, and thankfully she was alive!

Would she remain alive? How grave were her injuries? Where was the blasted horse? And how in damnation would he find a doctor way out here? Just what the hell had Samantha been doing out here?

But she'd kissed him back. Wait, she used her tongue; she'd learned that from him.

His mind was racing. Delirium caused by hypothermia soon to be followed by hypolectic shock, he diagnosed himself. He kept swimming as Samantha's response to his kiss had fired a brief hope within him. But that hope was dimming. He felt like he'd been swimming in this frozen lake for an eternity.

Then the most blessed sound he'd ever heard in all his thirty-one years greeted him. The enormous splash of Demon wading through the loch toward him. His lips were too numb to move. *Good boy!* He thought unable to articulate the words. He grabbed big handfuls of coarse horsehair as Demon nudged his stiff limbs, urging him to climb onto his broad back. Once on the horse's back, Light hoisted Samantha's limp form up onto the beast's broad withers. He secured her above the beast and then gratefully held on to her as Demon turned back toward shore. Light surreptitiously ran his hands up and down Samantha's limbs while the horse moved, checking for broken bones. Finding none, he cocked his head contritely up to the night sky.

"Thank you," he groaned. "But don't think for a minute that you and I are even. You still owe me one for taking both my parents but thank you just the same," he murmured. Then he slumped forward unconsciously, holding Samantha tightly as though she were his lifeline.

Chapter Twenty-Eight

The old man breathed a sigh of relief when his grandson's unconscious body crested the curve of the mountain. He was slumped over on his giant horse, clutching an equally unconscious Samantha in a tight grip on his lap. The old man had never thought he would lay eyes on either one of them again. But he'd been sending up prayers nonstop for the last two hours.

"Whoa," he said to the tired animal. He spoke to Demon in an ancient language that man and beast both understood. The horse stilled, his sides heaving laboriously -steam pumping from his nostrils from the cold lake.

Caelan relieved the horse of his twin burdens. After settling Samantha and his grandson by the fire and removing their wet, cold clothes, then he returned to care for the horse.

He dried Demon thoroughly with a flannel cloth .and then let the tired animal graze nearby. This day, Demon had saved most of what was left of the old Scot's family. He allowed his gratitude to show as he cared for the beast lovingly drying him. Lastly, he fed Demon extra oats from his own saddlebags. Caelin leaned his head against the horse's massive forelock, communicating his gratitude.

Satisfied that Demon was well cared for, he turned his attention to his grandson and Samantha. Caelin gathered leaves for a healing tea. Because of her long exposure to the elements, Samantha was feverish. She suddenly began thrashing violently, and she was hot to the touch. Using vines, he tied her to Lights still form to keep her from harming herself further. After a few minutes, she stilled. The lady might never forgive him for the damage to her virtue as she lay naked beneath a flannel blanket tied with vine to his grandson. But he had far more weighty matters to contend with than her modesty, he had to save her life.

Her fever was high, and he knew he had to save, or his grandson might never forgive him. He dried her still wet hair by the fire and then tilted her head up gently to help her sip the healing tea leaves. She choked and spat out the bitter brew but a little managed to make its way down. Then he unwrapped her makeshift bandage and applied salve to the bruises. He then did the same to Light.

After attending to his grandson, he sat down to do his vigil, watching over them, knowing he had done all he could to save their lives. The rest was up to the heavens. He pulled out his beloved instrument from his saddlebags and played his bagpipes pouring his feelings into every note. His melancholy song could be heard wailing across the mountain peaks till early morning.

He ministered to Light and Samantha for two days. After the second day, her fever broke. *Thanks be to the heavens!*

Lord Light woke first from his ordeal, complaining of the freezing cold even though it was a balmy day, and then he went back into a deep sleep.

On the morning of the third day, the old man went to the nearest dairy farm to borrow clothes and slippers for the young couple and buy supplies to break their fast. He knew they would wake up ravenous. He also sent word to Evansdale Manor that the young miss was all right.

All his searching couldn't yield any clothes that would fit the big frame of his grandson. The Scot had an extra shirt in his saddlebag and an extra kilt. It was time the young buck got back into a kilt. *Then maybe he'd cooldown on some of his hoity-toity sassenach ways,* MacDonald chuckled to himself, imagining his grandson's ire at being back into a kilt.

Chapter Twenty-Nine

Samantha reluctantly walked beside Light as they approached the posting inn as she hadn't wanted to stop there. After her ordeal, all she wanted was to head straight back to the manor. The harrowing events of the past few days had left her homesick for Evansdale. She longed to get back home as quickly as possible to soothe her raw emotions. But Light had insisted they stop at the inn for the night, he insisted that she looked pale and in need of rest.

He sent word to Evansdale Manor to expect them the next day before the noon meal, and he assured her family that she would be properly chaperoned. He hired the services of a local dairy farmer's daughter to act as Samantha's chaperone. Samantha didn't like him managing her in this way, but oddly his over-handed manner also allowed her mind to relax and focus on getting stronger.

Light's kilt swung against her dress as they walked into the inn. In her short acquaintance with him, he had never worn a kilt. Yester-eve he had.

He had looked unsure when his grandfather had shoved the kilt at him. It was clear that Light had no choice but to wear it as the sharp rocks of the loch had ripped through all the necessary places of his trousers, which now looked little better than rags. He hesitated a few seconds longer, shrugged, and stoically pulled the kilt over his broad legs.

Samantha had to admit that he looked quite handsome in it.

All the ladies at the posting inn seemed equally mesmerized by him. She could hear them whispering about him as they passed.

"I hear them is Highlanders. Look at him walk," one lady said in London slang

"I've heard tell these Highlanders don't wear nothing under them their kilts," said a snaggletooth crone as she laughed uproariously, studying Light and his grandfather both in matching kilts.

Samantha's eyes went wide as saucers when she heard that. She discreetly tried to look down at his kilt. He noticed the direction of her eyes and smiled knowingly down at her.

Light did not, in fact, have on anything under the kilt. He was as bare as a bone.

Reading the question in her too expressive eyes, he saucily said to her, "A penny for your thoughts?"

Startled hazel eyes flew up to his face, and she turned a bright red and looked away.

His rich baritone voice broke out in deep laughter, and Samantha blushed, looking up at him and then looking away. She steadfastly refused to meet his eyes, unsure what he was finding so amusing, but she suspected that he had some inkling about what she had just been thinking.

Their short walk led them to the inn entrance, and he held open the door for her. She noticed that his usually cool and diffident demeanor had transferred to a cocky swagger, and she smiled despite herself.

Much later that evening, after she'd rested, eaten, and changed clothes in the private room Light had reserved for her, she felt much better and was glad that he'd insisted they stop for the night. Her not so diligent chaperon kept forgetting about her charge and was even now enjoying the attention from the gentleman downstairs. It occurred to Samantha to object, but the simple girl was tiresome, constantly pestering Samantha for all the glamorous details of London society.

Samantha's thoughts strayed again to Light. *How had he known where to find her in that vast Loch?* Also, he had been right to insist they stop for the night, as she was quite weary. The only downside of the evening was that he had caught her staring at his kilt twice since dinner, and every time he saw her, he resumed his cocky swagger.

He had ordered a hot bath for her tonight, and she was beyond grateful for his thoughtfulness. After the boys had dumped the last bucket of hot water into the big round tub, she quickly barred the door and began to undress.

Drat! She hopped on one foot and twisted about this way and that. She couldn't get the laces off her bodice as they were tied tightly at the back. A tat-tat sounded on the window outside her room. As she tiptoed over to it, Light's face zoomed in through one of the square window panes. Samantha let out a sharp squeak, then clamped her hand over her mouth.

"What are you doing here?" she whispered.

"Don't be afraid," he breathed.

Her large hazel eyes tensed, but she didn't scream. Instead, she opened the window and looked around. No one seemed to be anywhere in sight. He had climbed the trellis to reach her second-story room.

She eyed him warily.

"Your chaperone doesn't seem too attentive," he explained. "I thought you could use some help with your ties."

She looked blankly at him as if he were speaking a foreign language.

"Can I come in?" he said hurriedly. "It wouldn't be good for me to be caught outside your window."

She hesitated.

"I promise, I'll leave straight away as soon as your ties are loosened."

Samantha looked down the window and back up at Light's face before she hurriedly ushered him inside in case they were seen. He leaped in like a cougar and closed the window curtains.

"May I?" he said, pointing to the back of her dress.

Samantha stepped away. "You should leave. This is most irregular…" she started to say, but then she remembered him lifting her out of the loch. She remembered him carrying her out of the water tenderly like some broken doll as she clung to him. His strength, his warmth, and his posture had been protective like an avenging angel. He had fought the depths of the loch to find her and almost lost his own life.

Some fledgling bond seemed to hatch between them at that moment as they looked at each other, remembering their ordeal. Tender emotion showed in his gray eyes. Gone was the cold ice king, who had loomed over her in that terrifying dungeon; (cold, aloof, distant). In his place was her rescuer, warm, earthy, kind and all males.

She felt inexplicably warm and shivery, as he continued looking at her. Heat was spreading through her skin. *What was its source? Was she feverish? But her fever had broken yesterday morning. Then why was she so hot?*

She swayed. She didn't see him move, but he was suddenly by her side. She didn't know how or why, but she instinctively pressed closer to him, her eyes floating to his lips. He was still, but she felt the tension in him.

"I'm trying to be noble here, Samantha," he croaked through suddenly dry lips. "But all my good intentions will flee if you look at me like that again."

Samantha nodded absently, hearing his words, and agreeing with them. *What had he tasted like?* She'd been feverish, but she remembered them kissing in the loch. She ran her hand along the back of her collar; she was getting hot again.

She heard him take a long deep breath and close his eyes. He seemed to be having some profound inner struggle.

"I think it's best you turn around, and let me undo your stays. We need to do this now while I can still walk out of here," he moaned.

Samantha dutifully turned around slowly. She felt his long, firm fingers unhooking and untying the strings of her stay. He obviously knew his way around a woman's intimate clothing; he let her out of her garments faster than any lady's maid could have.

He stepped back and turned around, giving her privacy. She shucked out of the garment and tiptoed to the tub, looking quickly over her shoulder to make sure he wasn't peeking. He stood immobile, facing away from her. A soft sigh escaped her as she sank gratefully into the warm water, submerging her head. Rivulets of water ran down her dewy skin, soaking her waist-length hair. She soon forgot about him as she began to relax in the warm water, curling her toes in pleasure.

Drat! She'd forgotten the bathing rags on her bed. Light seemed to have some sort of sixth sense because, at just that moment, he looked up at her, almost as if he'd heard her unspoken thoughts. He looked over at her bed, seeing the bathing rags and the lavender soap.

"May I hand it to you?" he asked with a lopsided grin.

Samantha wasn't sure what he found so amusing, but she was helpless to deny him. She needed the soap. She nodded jerkily, and he sprang into action, fluidly grabbing the bathing implements. But rather than hand them to her, he dipped them in the water and lathered them generously, and, without being asked, began to make soothing circles along her back, the cloth sliding smoothly over her spine.

Samantha's thoughts warred with each other. *The inappropriateness! But oh, it felt so good.* He smelled of starch and soap and a unique, clean smell all of his own. He engulfed her and surrounded her, his firm fingers working magic on her back. She was melting; that delicious heat was back, and it was traveling down her spine, spreading in her abdomen. She felt like purring as a delicious laziness was settling in her bones.

He stopped suddenly, shaking his head as if clearing it from a fog. "I want you, Samantha he purred, but I don't want you like this. You are just days away from a head wound. I want to win you honorably. I should leave."

She turned around to face him, and their eyes clashed. She was shocked to realize that she didn't want him to leave. She'd never wanted anything more than for him to stay.

Then Patricia's words floated up to the surface of her mind, and she faltered.

He tilted her chin up. "What is it?"

She tried to withdraw her chin, but he didn't allow it. "Tell me," he urged.

She searched his eyes for a long moment and then took a deep, shuddering breath. "Did you hit her? Patricia, I mean. Did you beat her?" Samantha challenged him.

Light closed his eyes. "Is that what she told you? Is that why you ran and ended up in the loch?"

Samantha didn't respond. She didn't have to. Light already knew.

He took a long, steadying breath. "I'm to blame for what

happened between Patricia and me. She was in love with me, and I took it for granted. I ended our affair in a way that wasn't fair to her. She hated me for it, and she had every right to, but I never hit her. I never laid a hand on her in anger. After what you saw in that blasted dungeon, I know you don't believe me. I've made so many mistakes, and I don't deserve your trust, but I'm asking for it anyway. Please believe me that I never hit Patricia. Everything I've done has always been with a willing partner."

She searched his eyes for so long he lost count of the minutes.

At last, she responded. "You're right," she whispered huskily. "You should leave." she said. He nodded jerkily and then left out the window, the same way he'd come in.

Chapter Thirty

Lord Light took a deep centering breath. He deliberately calmed himself down. Something was not right, but he couldn't find what it was. After years of repressing his feelings, he was now learning to use his intuition better. But it was very rusty. It came in starts and stops, and in times like now, he just wasn't able to read it, but he felt something.

"Damn it!" He bit back a curse and tried again for calm.

He cleared his mind as his grandfather had suggested on the mountain, but it didn't work. His sense of unease grew as he felt Samantha approach. She had sent around a note at breakfast with her chaperone, Marisol, that she needed an audience with Light at teatime this afternoon. Ever since the note had been delivered that morning, some four hours hence, little spurts of unease had grown inside of him.

He had arrived at the tea room in the inn a half-hour earlier than expected. The room had a magnificent view of the majestic mountains surrounding the lake. The sight of those tall, imposing mountains rising to the heavens had always seemed to calm him. He'd hoped for that effect again today, but sadly the unease within him did not die down.

He turned and watched Samantha approach, hoping, as she walked toward him, to find some clues as to why she wanted to see him here. Her eyes were downcast, and she held herself very rigidly and held her head a little too stiff. Something in her was triggering a sense of unease in him. She was agitated, and he was picking up on it. He locked his eyes further on her face and paid attention to her every expression. His focus must have been palpable because she looked up, met his eyes, and then looked away. Warring energy slid across his gut at her reaction.

She had some bad news to tell him. He noted it but kept his focus on her and smiled, trying to lighten the mood. Marisol had just brought in the tea tray a few moments before her lady's entry.

Light bowed to Samantha and reached for her hand. She reluctantly released her hand to him, her fingers stiff. He searched his memory for anything that could be amiss. As far as he could recall, they had been on the verge of becoming lovers last night. He sensed her passion for him had been real right up until the moment Patricia was brought up. She wanted him; her body told him so. Oh, he knew that women could be liars, especially beautiful women, but something very real was developing between them. He had no doubts that whatever was causing this tension in her, they'd work it out together.

He placed a reassuring kiss upon her hand and admired her startling beauty once again. He wondered if he'd ever get used to the effect she had on him.

Her hands were cold; the nervous energy in her skin snaked around his gut again. This time, he ignored it, telling his body that everything was fine between him and Samantha. *Wasn't it?* He desperately hoped it was because as he watched her impassive features while she poured his tea, he suddenly realized how dear this woman was to him. She was his, and he was finally ready to admit to himself that he loved her; and had probably loved her for a long time now. The image of her lying in the loch, cold and lifeless, came unbidden to his memory. When he thought that she could have been dead, he'd felt more despair inside himself than he had at any time in his life, even during the loss of both of his parents. He wasn't sure he could survive the loss of Samantha, and he never wanted to find out.

Why won't she look at me? He thought, *why won't she smile?* The unwelcome thoughts came unbidden but he pushed it aside.

"How was your ride on Demon?" he asked. The tense silence was almost his undoing, and he was desperate to break it.

She stopped pouring the tea, looked at him as if she had just realized he was in the room, and then went back to pouring her tea as if he hadn't spoken. Some long minutes later, after she had added two lumps of sugar to her tea and a dollop of cream, she settled in her chair and crossed her ankles carefully.

She finally deigned to answer. "It was a bit of a herring ride," she said. "He is a very spirited and short-tempered animal." She paused meaningfully and looked at Light as if to say, *sort of like his owner...* But she didn't make this statement; she just left it hanging in the air.

For that, he was grateful. He didn't want to be compared to some fairly respectable horse with good breeding and a lot of wildness.

She then went on to describe her ride in some detail. Light found to his amazement that he enjoyed all the sides of her personality. She was like a diamond with multiple sides. He'd seen glimpses of an extremely passionate nature, but at times like this, when she chose to be cool, she could match or even outdo his own coldness. That was saying a lot. It was rather intriguing trying to melt the arch coldness of this side of her personality. It was like finding a frozen pond but discovering a hot bubbling spring beneath it. That thought of a bubbling brook took him on a mental journey. He imagined the two of them in a hot spring, surrounded by water, naked, feasting on each other. He trained in his wild imagination with effort

There wasn't a hint of warmth to be found in her now, which added to the tension in his already tight muscles.

"Your note said you had something you wanted to discuss?" he prodded, wanting to get the meat of the matter over with so he could deal with it and then relax with her. His nerves were wearing thinner than they had in a long time.

The coolness suddenly left her, and she couldn't seem to still her hands. They fluttered about of their own accord. She set the teacup down, rather than risk dropping it; a faux pas Light instinctively knew she couldn't have tolerated. Her hands continued to dance, fluttering to her knees and then her hair. She began toying with the pearls at her neck, grasping them tightly. The pleasant cleavage peeking below the pearls took his thoughts on another pleasant journey, and again he reigned in his wild thoughts. *Focus! He admonished himself.*

Soon she clasped her hands to her lap, and then her toes began to tap. Light saw her deliberately still her nervous limbs by force of will. She turned to him, straightening her spine and in a clear, cool voice that didn't match her nervous energy, she spoke.

"Yes, I did, My Lord, I called you here today to inform you that I have decided to decline your offer of marriage. I have determined that you and I will not suit." She lifted her chin a fraction higher, loftily. "I have accepted the proposal of Rigsby. I have written ahead to Evansdale informing him of my acceptance. I am to become his wife."

Chapter Thirty-One

The room became completely still as they both stared at each other, her words were like a pronouncement that filled the space and hung in the air. To his credit, Light showed no emotion, though he was sure that at just that moment, his heart was breaking in pieces. His body had tried to warn him, but he still felt completely unprepared for what he'd just heard. *Why? He wondered.* Things had been going so well between them.

Hadn't they?

Don't do this to me, he thought silently. *Don't do this to us.*

He hadn't spoken the words out loud, but she tilted her head toward him as if she'd heard them anyway. With all the coolness gone now, again from her, she jumped out of her seat, unable to keep still. She paced. Her unease was evident, which confused him all the more. *Was this her decision, or was someone making her do this?*

He set his untouched tea down on the immaculate serving tray and crossed to the other side of the larger room to pace. He didn't want to be too near her at the moment as the raw pain from her words made it too painful.

He imagined her in someone else's bed as someone else's wife, and the thought caused a searing pain inside his chest. They were both lost in their separate thoughts, feeling the same pain in two bodies.

He was pacing by the window, and she was pacing by the hearth. The sun chose that exact moment to shine brightly into the room, making fun of their dark thoughts. He did not feel in control enough of his emotions to speak, and his pride would not allow him to beg.

Inwardly he begged her to reconsider; he was rendered mute by his pride (imprisoned in his despair).

"My Love, why are you doing this?" He thought silently to himself.

She stopped and turned toward him, misery written on her beautiful face. *Because, I have to.*

At first, he thought she'd spoken the words out loud, but she hadn't. And yet he'd heard them, all the same, inside himself. He shook his head. *Was he becoming unhinged?* He dismissed the worrisome thought. *Were they communicating the same way they had when she'd almost died in that damned loch?* It seemed as if tense situations involving death, danger or despair seemed to connect a bridge between the two of them, allowing them to feel each other's emotions. He wasn't hearing her thoughts as much as he was feeling them but they came through as clear as if she'd spoken out loud.

Like a drowning man, he wasn't above using any life raft that the universe seemed desirous to bring to him. He summoned all the love he felt for her into his body, he desperately hoped she could feel it. But nothing happened, and they each resumed their pacing.

"Oh!" Samantha suddenly clenched her midriff with trembling hands.

Light was at her side in a thrice. "What is wrong?" he said urgently, scanning every part of her that was visible to him, looking for injury.

She shook her head, tears silently streaming down her face. "I'm not hurt," she said. "I just feel…"

"What?" he asked anxiously, holding her close, unable to stop himself. "What do you feel?"

"You," she said. "I feel you. It's like I can feel your heart." She then seemed at a loss for words as she stood there trembling.

Chapter Thirty-Two

Lord Light woke up the next morning to a dark, dreary day. A day that matched his emotions. The woman he loved was going to marry another man. He had no idea what the hell he was going to do about it, but he knew that regardless of who she married, he would still love her. He'd waited a score of years to open up his heart to love, and now his heart was open, and it stubbornly refused to give up. He knew he would still love her whether she married him or someone else.

"*Sad*," he mumbled to himself. "*You're sad*." he chided his heart.

Love was sad.

He would likely live to an old age, and when he died, he'd still be in love with Samantha. Or, if he were lucky, he'd die from loving her, he thought bleakly as he rubbed the pain in his chest.

"Great," he grumbled to himself. *The woman I love is marrying another man, and I can't turn off my feelings for her which means I'm destined to love somebody else's wife for the rest of my life. Wonderful!*

He was tempted to be angry with God but ultimately ruled that one out. It wouldn't make a difference in the end, and sometimes if one was very lucky, the old boy in the sky came through once in a while. He'd seen it happen a time or two, and recently, he'd seen it happen when Samantha's life had been saved at the loch.

"I need help again!" he said in a loud voice. He cast a

skeptical glance at the gray clouds up above. Are you there? "If you could hurry the hell up though this time, that would be helpful," he complained. "Her wedding is in less than a week."

He glanced up again at the cold sky; he was becoming unhinged, he decided. He was officially going mad, he diagnosed himself.

To suit his vanity at being cast aside for another man, he got up and dressed carefully. He did it himself since he didn't have a valet, Simon was at Evansdale (evidently having better luck than Light was since Simon and Esther seemed to be an item these days). Being cast aside was something that never happened to Light in all his dealings with the fairer sex. He was usually the caster, not the castee, and he now felt very sorry for all the hearts he'd broken. He resolved to make a trip to the best florist in London upon his return to make amends to all his former lovers. Now that he'd tasted rejection, he realized how bitter of a pill it was.

He wrote a letter to his valet to bring him more kilts from home. The men in his family, the Highlanders, wore these kilts when they went to battle. There was no greater battle to win in one's life than the battle for love. In his own way, he'd fight for Samantha.

Chapter Thirty-Three

Samantha turned her silky head toward Light. She was surrounded in the warm cocoon of Light's entire body, enclosed in waves upon waves of the heat that flooded her. Like a moth to a flame, she turned fully toward his chest and wrapped her small arms around his massive torso. A fire burned low in the grate, illuminating his harsh features. He looked like he had been sculpted out of marble but to her he made her feel warm and safe.

She purred and purred again, deep in her throat, and the sound brought him closer. Their lips met of their own accord as if they couldn't bear to be separate, and he nibbled on her lower lip as if starving for the taste of her. Samantha lifted herself higher on his body, her tongue coming out shyly to taste him. The sensations were delicious and overwhelming. The heat of him under the hard satin of his skin, the smoothness of his muscles, the incredible softness of his lips.

She moaned again as his hands surrounded her, making soothing circles on her back. She was lost completely. She inhaled deeply, the scent of his sandalwood soap tickling her nose pleasantly, she needed something only he could provide, but what?.

"Light, please," she breathed his name. "Please." She wasn't sure what she was asking for.

"Miss, are you all right?" Marisol's tiny voice filled the space.

Samantha jerked upright, her heartbeat racing. She felt

disoriented. She was in her bedroom at the manor.

It had been a dream. But still, she couldn't help glancing around the room as there was a part of her that was looking for Light. *A dream? But it had felt so real.*

Marisol was looking at Samantha as if she was certain her mistress had lost her wits.

She had no idea how right she was, Samantha thought.

"I'm fine, Marisol" Samantha smiled reassuringly to ease the little maid's worry lines. "It was just a dream." Neither of them missed the note of wistfulness in Samantha's voice. *A most wondrous dream,* she thought silently to herself.

A knock sounded on her bed chamber door.

"What in all that is holy is going on now, Marisol asked?" her voice huffed as she crossed the chamber to answer the door.

"Who is it?" she asked, sounding very put upon.

Samantha was contrite. She really shouldn't be keeping the servants up all hours of the night. Their days were long enough without having to lose sleep at night. She vowed to make it up to Marisol.

She pulled the covers up to her chin, curious as to who could be at her door at such an ungodly hour.

"It's Litchfield," a strong masculine voice said from the other side of the door. "Is your mistress all right? I felt…" he paused as he seemed to be having difficulty finding the words to explain what he felt. "I felt something amiss," he said lamely in a low voice to Marisol from the other side of the door.

Her maid looked at Samantha, frightened. "Miss, it isn't proper for him to be here at this hour with you in your nightclothes."

Samantha didn't seem to hear. She was lost in thought. *What had Light felt?* From his voice, he seemed as unsure about it as she. Whatever it was, she herself was unsure. *Could he have felt her dream? Like she had felt his despair when she'd announced she was marrying Rigsby?*

"Open this door!" he demanded in his characteristically arrogant voice.

The little maid jumped and looked at Samantha. Samantha, more curious than not by his appearance at her door at this time of night, especially so soon after her dream, ordered the maid to let him in. She could not have put into words her emotions at that moment, and she was chagrined to realize that she was anticipating seeing him again.

The maid hesitated.

"Go ahead," she whispered to Marisol. "You're here as a chaperone of sorts. Open the door."

The door opened on silent, well-oiled hinges. Light emerged through the door, his hair standing straight up as if he'd been running frustrated hands through all the while. His feet were bare as if he'd been in too great of a hurry to don his shoes.

As soon as the door opened, his eyes flew to Samantha's face. He inspected her carefully, and then his gaze traveled around the room. It was only because she was staring at him full on that she saw the small sigh of relief he expelled after examining the room.

He dragged his eyes back to her face, and then as if something amusing had just occurred to him, he smiled heatedly at her and gave her a saucy look. Samantha, for some reason she couldn't understand, blushed hotly under that too knowing look.

But her voice did her proud; it was steady and cold as she said in her best imitation of an outraged female, "Are you quite done gawking at me, My Lord?"

He inhaled sharply as if she'd struck him, and he shook his

head to clear it. A nerve ticked in his jaw as he straightened slightly, but he maintained that sassy look in his eyes as if he knew a very charming secret.

"My apologies, my Lady," he drawled slowly. "I beg your pardon for intruding upon your sleep. It is my hope that your dreams were pleasant." There was a velvety thickness that lowered his words to an almost caress.

The tiny maid stood speechless, looking back and forth between the two of them as if watching a play. Samantha knew this entire conversation was improper and that Light's very presence at her door was borderline scandalous especially in light of her recent engagement to Rigsby.

However, to her everlasting shame, she couldn't find the space to care. Truth be told, she wanted him there. She wanted all the things that had been occurring in her dream to happen in reality and with him. Her body was still humming from that dream even though a quarter of an hour had passed.

Light chuckled low in his throat as if reading every one of her thoughts, causing Samantha to fidget and squirm uncomfortably and then blush furiously. Her face was so hot, she resembled a ripe tomato.

What did he know? she wondered. The worry made her bite her bottom lip. *Why had he shown up so soon after her dream? What did he mean when he said he felt something? Could he? Was it possible?* That horrified her.

Her eyes flew to his face, and their eyes collided; hers shocked and questioning, his swaggering and self-assured. Samantha internally groaned at the implications of that look. It was all too confusing for her to grasp; the intimacy of the dream and her panic that he knew.

She retreated inside herself, reaching for her mask of cool

hauteur as a defense. She coolly raised the blanket higher under her chin.

"Thank you for your concern. As you can see, my Lord, I am quite all right, and I trust that you know your way out," she said in the coldest voice she could muster.

Light smiled lazily, nonplussed, and nodded agreeably. He gave a slow, exaggerated bow. "I am ever at my Lady's service." He turned and left without a backward word or glance.

The little maid looked at his retreating figure in wonderment, and then she closed the door and leaned against it, her small hand fluttering to her chest. Samantha felt the same way. She slid lower in the bed until her head hit the pillow, and then she snuggled under the covers in wonderment.

"Me thinks, he knows too much…" she muttered to herself.

Chapter Thirty-Four

Light was fit to be tied. Nothing, absolutely nothing was going right since his return to the manor. Samantha's blasted engagement to Rigsby had him feeling sour and put upon (more than he liked to admit). He'd woken up last night not sure what had pulled him out of sleep. *"Light, please"* he'd heard Samantha's voice in his mind's eye as clear as day. "Please what?" He wondered grumpily. Tearing out my heart isn't enough, what did she want next, his liver. Nonetheless he got out of bed intent on checking on her; her safety was his chief concern (always). *"Please."* He'd heard it gain more intensely this time, it sounded like she was in pain, he took off at a dead run forgetting to don his shoes. After almost breaking the door down to gain entry he scratched his head to find her safely ensconced in bed alone, with no one about but a tiny little maid but his beloved was blushing furiously her eyes finding it difficult to meet his straight on. He puzzled over the scene before him for some seconds then realization dawned on him, and he chuckled. He hadn't found sleep for the rest of the night. Even a cold dunking in the freezing lake at dawn hadn't helped. Now sour tired lovelorn and fidgety he stood under the scowling scrutiny of an irritated Simon that morning. "If his lordship would but still his constant movements for a short moment then perhaps, I can get this ensemble fitted on you before sundown tomorrow." Simon lamented trying again and failing to fasten Light's cravat. Light's normally acerbic tongue was lethargic today, Light simply nodded and stilled his fidgety limbs.

His valet dressed him meticulously for the last competition.

Today's competition was supposed to be the tiebreaker. Whoever won today's competition was the overall winner. None of the guests knew, however, that the last competition was simply a formality; the lady in question, Samantha, had already made her choice. But the competition would go forward as planned for the entertainment of the guests and the local gentry that had been invited weeks ago. A part of Light's heart longed to retreat back to his London Mansion where he could lick his wounds in private. Losing Samantha to Rigsby was bad enough but watching Rigsby swagger about the manor with that self-satisfied smirk on his face was a kettle of a different fish, and one Light had difficulty swallowing. He longed to wipe that smirk off Rigsby's face. To that end he'd start by winning today's competition.

A sinister side of Light's wanted some small retribution for having lost his girl. "These lower lords hadn't seen the last of Lord Light, not by a longshot," he mumbled to himself. Truth to tell, he should have been declared the winner of these games long ago. But by some underhanded trickery (probably by Rigsby), the competitions had progressed while Light and Samantha were away. Each game Light had missed had counted as a forfeit. Still, Light had no regrets; he had been busy saving his beloved's life. Samantha meant more to him than all the wins in the world.

But Light would still compete in this last competition and win, and *then what*? He wondered, suddenly feeling lonely. The prospect of facing the long, lonely years ahead without Samantha —being all alone momentarily overwhelmed him. He'd have nothing to comfort him over the coming years; nothing other than his wealth and his mansion. *Was it enough?* He'd always thought it was before. *But now?* Now he wasn't so sure. Light pounded on his chest again to still the longing. He put on a stiff upper lip and headed out to the greens.

He was unruffled at the outcome of today's games. He was guaranteed to win. Today's sport was one in which he excelled in exceptionally well. His late father had been a champion in the sport and had taught his only son well.

The men would be split up into two teams; Light and Rigsby were the leaders of their respective teams. A large patch of grass west of the grounds was the playing area. Large white nets staked on wooden pegs were set up on opposite ends of the field. The players had to get a ball into the net on the other side of the opponent's field while riding a horse and hit the ball with a flat club while on horseback. Speed, agility, and great horsemanship were needed to win. Light had all three, and among his peers in London, he was a god of this game. He never lost. It also didn't hurt that his horse, Demon, was two hands taller than most of his competitors. The mere sight of Demon on the greens had the mares trembling (whether in fear or excitement Light didn't know or care; either one worked to his benefit).

*

The staff pushed Samantha's grandmother in her wooden chair to the head of the greens in the area set up for spectator seating, so that she could judge the competition. Samantha looked radiant in a forest green day gown, with gold fichu overlaid over the bodice. The benches where the spectators sat were full, and it seemed the whole of the country folks had come out to watch the sport. Gents were discreetly placing wagers, and children hopped up and down, trying to see over the shoulders of elders.

Light walked toward his designated spot when he heard the groomsmen grousing with each other.

"Oh, dear," squealed the head groom. "This part of the estate is covered in mud from the morning rains. We won't be able to get the chair across to take her ladyship to her place of honor."

"Take me back," ordered the grandmother. "I don't want my chair to get stuck in the mud." The inept men ended up getting her wooden chair stuck deeper in the mud.

Light sighed, watching their machinations as they all struggled with the chair. He noticed that Samantha looked alarmed as she watched on. "Allow me, ma'am," |Light said gallantly to the grandmother, stepping forward, his gear swinging against his long legs. His dark wavy black hair was slicked back and tied in a perfect queue at his nape. He looked dapper, and he knew it. He caught a stray assessing glance as Samantha looked him up and down and then she glanced away shyly. She looked flushed, especially when he caught her surveying him appreciatively. He was satisfied; his pride could not have tolerated her indifference.

He turned toward her grandmother and tucked the lady's shawl securely around her slim waist. He lifted her in his arms and began crossing the mud with her, high on his chest. Her groomsmen now managed to get the chair out of the mud and followed the trio. Samantha was ineffectively trying to calm her grandmother down from having an apoplexy at the perceived afront by Light.

"Put me down this instant, you big oaf!" she groused.

"Grandmother, he is only trying to help. He is just being gallant." Samantha sighed, peeking at Light from over her grandmama's head.

"Helpful, my big toe!" said her grandmere. "He's a

neanderthal. Imagine the nerve of whisking me up from my chair as if I were a sack of potatoes or a loaf of bread?" But nevertheless, she eventually subsided under Samantha's cajoling.

Light looked askance at the grandmother as he hefted her light frame across the greens. *Did the lady ever eat?* he thought worriedly. *She weighed less than a sack of flour.*

"We've cleared the mud, Light," she complained at length. "You can put me down now, for God's sake."

Light was enjoying the newfound camaraderie between the three of them, and he was uncharacteristically loath to return to their previous hostilities. Besides, it seemed Samantha was touched by how he was caring for her grandmother. He needed all the points he could get where Samantha was concerned, so he carried on as he was.

"It's only a few more steps, ma'am," he assured her. "Besides, I'm not entirely sure of the capability of those young men you call groomsmen after what I witnessed. Why they almost had you face down in that mud, and besides, I would prefer to see to your well-being myself."

Samantha beamed, at his words but the old lady harrumphed.

Light ordered the men to set the chair in a place of honor—close enough for the lady to see everything but far away enough not to be trampled. He instructed that it be placed just so—so that it was not directly in the sun, and when he was finally satisfied, he set her down carefully. He bent to arrange her shawl around her shoulders, but she slapped his hands away.

"I can manage myself," she huffed as Samantha took a seat on the bench next to her grandmother.

Light stepped back and bowed gallantly to her. He heard her muttering as he walked away but couldn't make out all the words though the phrase "impudent pup" stood out clearly. To his discomfort, he discovered that his boots were now soaked and crusted with mud. He tried to get into his saddle on Demon, but his foot kept slipping out of the stirrups. Once he was finally seated, he was still having difficulty maintaining his footing. These games required him to maintain a tight grip on the stirrups while he leaned low to the ground to hit the ball accurately with his club. However, his foot continued to slip from the stirrups when he changed position in the saddle. But there was no time to fetch his other boots.

Nicholas approached, looking fresh and clean in white linen pants, a white lawn shirt, and shiny black hessian boots that gleamed brightly in the sun. He looked questionably at Light's mud-encrusted boots. Light shrugged as if to say, 'Nothing can be done about it now, Old Boy. Let's just rally anyhow we can.'

Nicholas nodded, understanding the unspoken command.

With their heads bent low in earnest discussion, they spoke in lowered tones assessing their opponents and planning their strategy. Light looked up and caught a knowing smile from his grandfather in the spectator area. The old man had seen this pair plotting thusly often as lads. MacDonald was on a bench near Samantha's grandmother. Strangely the grandmother was smiling at something the old man had said. Light frowned as something about the pair disturbed him, but he couldn't figure it out. He turned his attention back to his cousin.

Rigsby came out at that moment looking striking in a red velvet tailored jacket, black trousers, and gleaming hessian boots. He looked smugly at Light, taking in his muddy boots. Without breaking eye contact with Light, Rigsby walked over to Samantha, lifted her to her feet, and gave her a full sensual kiss on the lips. His right hand slid down possessively onto her buttocks, squeezing suggestively lifting her slightly off her feet.

He then set her back on her feet and bowed elegantly to her while tipping his hand to Light in mock salute.

Samantha hastily sat down, flustered, chagrined, and red-faced.

Light saw red, then blue, and then green, so many emotions flooded his senses each one triggering a different color; he was red with rage, blue with sadness and green with envy all at once. To add insult to injury he was being mocked, to boot. To Light's everlasting shame, Rigsby's obvious attempt to anger him was working; it made him green with envy and red with fury, a dangerous combination.

"Have you heard a blasted word I've said?" Nicholas shook his cousin's big frame with both hands, trying to get his attention. "Alexander Ignore that bastard. He's trying to bait you." Nicholas could clearly see the fury and jealousy on Light's face.

"Well, it's working." Light ground out (a fist unconsciously forming at his side). He didn't take his eyes off Rigsby's swaggering form as Rigsby dusted his immaculate boots and climbed easily onto his horse unassisted. He smiled arrogantly back at Light, his long blonde hair blowing in the cool breeze.

"In a fair fight, he loses to you every time, and he knows it." Nicholas persisted, worried about Light's focus. Nicholas had never seen Alexander so furious. "His best chance at winning is trickery," Nicholas persisted.

The image of Rigsby's tanned hand sliding down Samantha's luscious derriere would not leave Light's mind. His sole desire at that moment was to wipe that smug grin off that pompous ass's face.

"Light, are you paying attention to the plan?" Nicholas hissed, getting furious. His cousin wouldn't have to worry about Rigsby because if he didn't get his head out of his arise and stop being baited, Nicholas himself would knock Light's block clean off. But Light kept staring at Rigsby, with a scowl etched on his brow.

"Think, man!" Nicholas warned. "Be cold. Do not get emotional. That's how people lose."

Light shook Nicholas' arm off of him. "The time for cold has ended." he ground out. He was hot. This was getting personal, and Light had a score to settle with Rigsby. The hand that had grabbed Samantha's derriere was his target. He decided he was going to club that arm with his club like a Mallett; consequences be damned.

Nicholas scowled fiercely at Light's back as they joined the lineup with their other team mates on their horses.

Light played the game as if his life depended on it, and by the first half, his team was up by 12 points. Rigsby and his horse had taken so many direct hits from Light's club that Rigsby had been forced to retire his first horse from the game and get a fresh mount. It was clear to everyone present that these two men had a personal score to settle. Whereas Light's anger had served him well in the first half of the game, lending his attacks a strength and agility that was unmatched, it proved to be his undoing in the second half.

Light lined up his shots perfectly. Rigsby realized that he personally was Light's sole target. Light seemingly didn't want to win the match as much as he wanted to smash Rigsby with his ball at every opportunity. Winning the game came second to Light. His primary desire was to whack away at Rigsby, nonetheless Light led his team to a 12-point lead with Rigsby's team at zero (a crushing defeat for Rigsby in the first half). In the next play, Light was supposed to hit his ball east to pass it to Nicholas, who was ready to receive the ball and score. But Light saw Rigsby in his sights, standing in the open. Forgetting the play and much preferring to inflict more physical injury on his nemesis, Light changed course and sent his ball flying straight at Rigsby's midriff with all the force he could muster.

Rigsby sneering with a knowing jeer as if he'd expected the move, easily side-swiped the hit and placed himself and his horse out of harm's way, all the while touching his forehead with two fingers in a mock salute.

"Check, mate," Rigsby mouthed to Light, followed by a victorious smirk.

Light understood the words but was immensely puzzled. His team was winning by 12 points, so what accounted for Rigsby's smug, self-congratulatory smile? By the time Light realized, (it was too late). The ball flew past Rigsby and, with a sickening thud, smacked Samantha's grandmother squarely in her forehead

The genteel ladies' mouths flew open in shock as she flipped over backward, her body flailing. Her skirts upended as she landed, and her head hit the ground with a solid whack. The entire assembly went silent, some even crossing themselves. All eyes turned to Light in shock as their jaws flew open.

Rigsby chose that moment to bow to Light in a mocking salute. Light felt a sickening sensation in his gut. *Was the lady dead?* He knew firsthand how much force he'd applied to that ball as he'd intended it for Rigsby. If she died, Samantha would never forgive him. *Oh, God,* thought Light, the full import of what he'd just done landing on him as he jumped down from his horse. All the players dismounted; each one took off their hat in respect of the lady waiting on one knee in frozen shock.

Eventually the spectators snapped out of their shock and began racing to the lady's still form. Rigsby continued to look at Light in mockery. However, Light did not respond; he now had bigger problems than Rigsby; Nicholas was headed straight for him, fury etched on his cousin's face.

"Now, Cousin," Light began placatingly putting his hands up in the air. "It was an accident."

Nicholas came nose to nose with Light and, with a menace Light hadn't seen in him since they were age 12, Nicholas buried his right fist in Light's gut. For all his slenderness, Nicholas was all muscle, and when he chose to, he could take down an elephant. This was a point he proved now as Light went down, the pain doubling him over instantly. To add pain to injury, as he lay doubled over on the greens, his head on the grass he caught Samantha's shocked expression as she looked on at him while he was curled up on the greens in a fetal position. *Drat- his humiliation was complete.*

Nicholas casually stepped over Light's prone position on the greens and let his handkerchief fall on Alexander's face. "Are you sure the time to be cold is over?" he inquired blandly as he walked away. "Because it looks like you just ended up with egg on your face?"

Humbled, Light got to his feet and limped off. The game resumed in his absence, and some short hours later, Rigbsy's team was announced as the winner (13-12). The name of the game was changed from pole ball to Rugby in Rigsby's honor. It would retain that name for years until Rigsby himself transferred the name to another favorite game he much preferred.

*

Doctors came in and out of her ladyship's rooms, but she remained unconscious. Back in his rooms, Light tried to hide his humiliation by sinking into a bottle of his good Scotch Whiskey and refusing to come downstairs but again nothing was going right. There was no more Scotch Whiskey. Really? He asked Simon. What next? "How did this happen Simon?" Light inquired.

"It's all finished, My Lord." his valet declared calmly. "Don't you remember that you gave away most of it to the staff in exchange for information?"

Light nodded belatedly. He was sure now that he had unwittingly descended into the seventh circle of hell—when would this house party end? "I was able to find some French Brandy," Simon interjected, trying to lighten the mood.

Light's morbidness was weighing them both down. "That swill?" Light huffed. "I wouldn't feed that to my dogs."

Simon shrugged, as if to say—have it your way—it's no skin off my back.

"All right, all right," Light conceded, stretching his long legs by his fireplace in his rooms. "Serve it to me. I might as well drink French Brandy. This day can't get any worse than it already is."

Chapter Thirty-Five

Later that night, after everyone had gone to bed, Light snuck into her ladyship's bed chamber. As he'd hoped she was alone, low candles burned on her night table, and warm blankets covered her still form. She was dressed like royalty in a gold and silver dressing gown where she lay still and regal on a silver pillow. Her black and gray hair was covered by a silk cap. An angry red bump was pronounced on her forehead. It had swollen until it was the size of a chicken egg.

Despair filled Light's heart. He pulled a nearby chair closer to her and bent his dark head in prayer, his handsome features solemn with regret. *Please don't die...* he rasped. *Please don't die.* He prayed silently and sat by her side. After an hour of silent vigil, he made a vocal appeal.

"God, I need your help again. If you could come through for me again, this time like you did when you saved Samantha? Please do it again. We'll be even this time. Please, God, don't let her die. Please. He continued to pour his heart out to God."

After a few more hours, Light eventually fell asleep, occasionally waking up to check on Samantha's grandmother. Nothing; she was as still as a grave. He dozed off to sleep again.

As the sunrise began its journey, he heard her ladyship begin to stir.

"What are you doing in here, Light?" She asked in a cantankerous voice, her watery gray eyes staring defiantly at him.

Light was momentarily disoriented as he woke up, chagrined

that he'd fallen asleep. "You're awake." He sighed. "Thank God." He ran tanned hands through his disheveled hair.

Something in the grandmother's expression softened, but she held it back, scowling instead. "Of course, I'm awake. How could I be talking to you if I wasn't?"

In that moment her cantankerous voice and sullen face were the most beautiful sights Light had ever seen. He'd thought that he'd never again have the pleasure of being dressed down by her ever again. He smiled happily—he was glad she was still alive to give him a hard time.

"No, ma'am," he said, adjusting the covers gently around her frail frame. "You wouldn't be able to. I'm just glad that you are awake… And talking, that is."

"Light, you're not making any sense. It's as if you were the one hit on the head instead of me. But you haven't answered my question. What are you doing here?"

He lowered his head in pain and shame. "I owe you an apology. I'm very sorry. I'm more sorry than I can express. I didn't intend "

She cut him off as a rare look akin to gentleness crossed her features. "You thought I was going to die," she said.

He nodded. "And you were praying for me." Again, Light nodded.

"The same way you prayed when Samantha was missing."

"Yes," he said.

"And God answered your prayer; that's how you found her."

Light was going to nod again but stopped part way. "Wait, how did you know that? No one was there, just Samantha and I, and I never told her."

She harrumphed. "Well, you said as much when you sat here last night."

"Last night? But you were unconscious. How did you hear?" He turned suspicious eyes in her direction, his brow going up. "Were you unconscious?" he inquired.

Knowing gray eyes as old as the earth looked through him and around him, but this time, they didn't seem to find him wanting. She nodded, satisfied. "No, I wasn't unconscious, but one doesn't get to know another's thoughts unless they appear to be asleep. You're not the only one with tricks up your sleeve, Light." Her smile took the heat out of the words.

He leaned back in his chair, strangely feeling lighthearted. "I'm sure I don't know what you mean, Ma'am. By the results of this house party, it is clear that whatever tricks I might have thought I had up my sleeve are nil. I've been outsmarted, outmanned, outmaneuvered, and outdone at every turn."

"Posh." She waved a dismissive hand. "You just let Rigsby get your goat is all. He knows how to push your buttons. He knows you're in love with Samantha, as we all do. When she approaches, you get that stupid look on your face, and you start swaggering around like a peacock. Rigsby uses her to get to you and being a man, of course, you're not too smart, so you let him."

Light didn't know how to feel about these statements. Most of them were disparaging, to say the least, but the lady was smiling as she spoke to them, and she was alive. "I'll let you get your rest, ma'am," he murmured.

"Not so fast, young man. Samantha is marrying Rigsby tomorrow. It's what I thought I wanted, but now I'm not so sure. You're everything I thought you were, but something has changed. I don't know for sure, but I think Samantha might love you in return, but she's scared. Something has spooked her. If you're the right man for her, you'll find the right words to make her trust you." She sat up and reached inside her bedside table, getting out a small pink and brown leather-bound book. "Give her this," she handed Light the book.

"You're helping me," he inquired incredulously, his perfectly arched aristocratic brows rising up in surprise.

"I'm not doing it for you," she grumbled. "I'm doing it for Samantha. It's a joint diary, the front is pink, and the back is brown. When I was newly married, I would write in it every night. I wrote on the pink side, then I'd hand it to Oliver, and he'd write on the brown side. We loved comparing each other's stories, and we always signed it the same way every night... confide in me semper."

Light translated. "Trust in me always."

"Yes." She nodded. She'll recognize that book, and she'll know if Ive given it to you that I must have had a change of heart. It won't guarantee you success but at least she'll hear you out. It will be up to you to find the right words.

"What are you doing in here!" Bart demanded, balancing a tea tray in two strong, tanned hands. Scowling fiercely at Light as if he wanted to knock his lights out.

Light looked up, startled.

"What is he doing in here, Grandmere? Hasn't he done enough?"

Light put his hands up then. "I deserve that," he said humbly. "I'll leave."

"Yes, you do deserve that, but I've forgiven you." She smiled. "Bart, stop barking at my guest and set up the tea on the table. As you can see, I'm fine. Now, get out of here, both of you. As you can see I'm perfectly fine. now let me enjoy my tea in peace."

Chapter Thirty-Six

Light stared at his reflection in the looking glass one last time before heading out to dinner. He was in much better spirits tonight than he had been for the past few nights. He'd eschewed from eating in the main dining room. Rather he'd had a small tray of food brought up to his rooms each night. But tonight, he chose to end his self-imposed exile. He expected to face some censure from the guests at tonight's dinner party. It was his first time in public since his ball had hit Samantha's grandmother in the head. But now that he knew the grand lady had forgiven him, he no longer cared about the criticism of the others. Samanthas and her grandmother's opinions were the only ones that held any weight with him. But he took pains with his ensemble tonight. He believed in looking resplendent whenever facing an unhappy crowd. As such he allowed Simon to take his time putting together this evening's ensemble. Dark wool merino trousers flowed elegantly around his tall frame. His white shirt was simple and framed his wide shoulders comfortably. The jacket was simply cut by his London tailor, the only touch of pretension was the embossed family crest on the collar of his jacket and his large signet ring on his pinky finger. He debated whether to remove the ring after all he was in the country at a small dinner party with less than a hundred in attendance. Belatedly, he decided to keep it on. He and Rigsby were in a war of sorts over Samantha and in war it never hurt to remind the enemy that Light ran a large dukedom (on the slim chance that the opponent being out ranked might have the good manners to withdraw). It was unlikely of course but one never knew. Satisfied with his appearance, he turned away from the looking glass and absently patted the diary that Grandmere had given him that morning, it was in an inside pocket inside his jacket, he hoped it would bring him luck when he talked with Samantha later that night after dinner. Whistling a merry tune, he strode to the top step and agilely ran down the stairs two at a time as fleet footed as a deer. He was grateful for the dim light at the bottom of the stairs because he was unable to hide his shock at what greeted him when he reached the bottom of the stairwell. A line of seven gentlemen in black evening clothes stood in the middle of the sitting room entrance in a straight row. They all were facing him, their features stoic and somber. He took a step toward them, offering a mild greeting. To a man, they all uniformly turned away, presenting him with their backs. They stood there like a line of soldiers, their backs to him, pretending he didn't exist. His stupefied expression was transfixed on his face. A cut direct. By seven gentlemen. They showed him by their mutual actions that they didn't consider him one of them, in their eyes, he wasn't a gentleman. Some of the seven were men he regularly did business with; others were clearly Rigsby cronies. Rigsby stood at the head of the line.

Seven gentlemen, his own peers, all turning their back on him, that had to be some kind of record. Light recognized Rigsby's stiff back at the head of the line. Even from the back Light could tell that Rigsby was very pleased with himself. Belatedly Light realized that these gentlemen were creating a buzz and some of the ladies agreed with their tough stance. Light was once again the center of attention. All eyes were locked on him to see how he would react. Several ladies turned sad eyes in his direction, feeling pity for him that he'd been ostracized; such pity of course was worse than the latter. He rather preferred the scorn than the pity. Fans started fluttering in quick succession, hushed whispers floating in the air. Light recovered his shock and closed his open jaw pulling the shutters over his eyes and leaning back on his heels casually. So, they meant to shame him, did they? He digested this tidbit while feigning a nonchalance he was far from feeling. Out of the corner of his eye, he spotted Nicholas walking into the dining room, fashionably late as usual, a snifter of scotch in his lean hands. Light's stomach clenched as he watched his cousin approach him while taking in the scene— their two eyes locked. They hadn't spoken a word to each other since Nicholas had punched Light in the gut over hitting a lady with a ball. With Nicholas chivalry was never dead. Light tightened his gut as he watched Nicholas approach, never breaking eye contact. These buffoon's and their insults Light could tolerate but if Nicholas joined the seven and turned his back on him Light knew his innards would crumble. *Et tu Brutae?* he wondered as Nicholas surveyed the scene, deciding which side to take, A cold expression filling Nicholas' youthful face, several ladies watched Nicholas as he surveyed the scene also wondering what side he would take. Uncharacteristically Nicholas sipped his drink loudly and then swaggered joyfully over to Light, feigning a slight drunkenness. Cuz you've got to try this new Scottish whiskey grandfather just had delivered today; as perfection goes it is superb. He clasped his cousin lightly on the back and handed over the drink. In a quick voice only Light could hear, he whispered, "Here drink this, you look like you could use it," he whispered for Light's ears only. Light looked straight into his cousin's eyes, expressing his gratitude. Nicholas nodded in acceptance. And just like that they were reconciled.

"Now what are we going to do about these fool?" Nicholas asked, indicating the seven.

Light took a long drink of the fine highland scotch savoring it slowly.

"I don't know," he said at length, smiling as if he was having the best time of his life. I'm just glad you're not over there standing with them." Light watched Samantha enter, her face wore a curious frown as she surveyed the scene, her concerned eyes flew to his own. He shrugged nonchalantly as if to say, "What else is new at this house party." She looked away and went to join a small group of girls that were quite obviously discussing Light and how his peers had quite literally turned their back on him. He could tell he was the topic of conversation by the way the girls kept peeking discrete looks at him from the top of their fans.

"Of course, I'm not standing with them," Nicholas replied. "Do I think you acted like an arise? Of course, I do; but you're my cousin, family first. Besides when I have a problem with someone, I prefer to settle the matter man to man. Public shaming is not my cup of tea."

Light nodded and decided to needle his cousin. "On that note cut, I forgot to tell you that you hit like a girl."

Nicholas' face froze and he snatched his drink back. That's not what I saw—he retorted jovially with saucy banter- "I had you laid out on your back in the dirt, I'd like to see a girl do that." Light signaled for a waiter. "Lucky shot, cuz, that's all it was—a lucky shot."

"Back to the matter at hand," Nicholas said, getting down to business indicating the seven with his drinking glass. "I have an idea." The two bent their heads closely. "Those yo-yo's (he indicated the seven) presently have the spotlight on them and I bet they're enjoying it. Let's turn the tables, we'll turn the spotlight off, we become the life of the party and those numb nuts will be forgotten by the assembly at large; the seven of them might as well diddle themselves where they stand (that's how bored they'll be) once no one is paying them any attention."

Light nodded intently to Nicholas, liking the plan he reached for another scotch as a white clad waiter handed him his drink. "But how exactly do we do that, cuz. Must I remind you that since I knocked our hostess unconscious at the games yester-eve, I am now persona non-grata, that is to say I'm currently a pariah. I couldn't draw a crowd even if I had a string."

Nicholas nodded in agreement. "Yes, Alexander, you sure do know how to draw enmity from a crowd; I'm surprised you've lived this long up to this point." Light shrugged and let Nicholas' barbs bounce off of him. He deserved it, he'd been acting like a first class ass ever since he met Samantha. As to your question Nicholas continued, "I'll have you know that I happen to be very well versed in the dramatic arts, I was the queen's favorite courtier at the French court. You might be a pariah cuz, but I'm not. And everyone knows the ladies are the life of the party. Bring the ladies to you, and you'll control the room. I'm going to bring the ladies out here to us. As for you, do try to be charming cuz." Nicholas looked skeptically at Light. As if to say, can you manage that?

Light sighed, answering the unspoken question. "Yes, I can be charming to the ladies Nicholas. Afterall, I am a Duke."

Yessss—Nicholas nodded—you are a Duke. He put emphasis on each vowel in the word Duke. "Now if you can just remember that then we can pull this off just fine" and with that sarcastic retort, Nicholas was off. "My ladies," Nicholas lamented to one chubby redhead maiden surrounded by her friends inside the sitting room. "Perhaps, you would be kind enough to help my cousin and I settle a debate." The ladies giggled instantly, becoming tongue tied by his handsomeness. Just like that he had their attention. "A debate" squealed Margo, her cheeks red as she stared at Nicholas with adoring eyes, her red curls bouncing.

"Whatever is the debate about Lord Nicholas" she inquired?

Nicholas placed a hand on his heart. "My cousin and I were debating on which of the three musketeers is the most dashing (is it Athos, Porthos or Aramis). To help you ladies decide my cousin, and I would love to do a small snippet of the play from each of the three characters"

"A play," squealed Marjorie, a lovely olive-skinned debutante at Margo's right. He lifted Margo's hand to his lips. "Would you help us settle the debate as well?" he inquired staring deep into her amber eyes.

"It would be a great honor to have a lady of your obvious taste settle the matter. She positivity glowed, "Why yes Lord Nicholas and my friends would love to help as well, wouldn't we ladies, a round of nods met the question. We love that play. It is so romantic," Margo declared. The girls all squealed in delight.

A thin brunette in a white virginal evening gown shyly stepped forward. "Lord Nicholas, is it true that you were in the French court and that you've performed for the queen at court." A hush fell over the ladies closest to him and other ladies nearby were also leaning in listening for his answer, while they pretended not to be listening. (But Nicholas saw their discrete movements).

He endeavored to include them as well, talking loudly for all to hear. "Ladies, let me tell you about the French court." He sighed dramatically, talking loudly for the room at large, "Follow me he instructed" and then taking Marjorie's hand in his left and Margo's hand in his right indicating with his head that the others must follow he led the way out of the sitting room past the seven men their backs still turned and out to main foyer by the grand staircase. Samantha excused herself from her relations and also followed Nicholas bringing her friends along. She guessed what Nicholas was up to and made a move to support him. All the young females in the sitting room exchanged curious glances at the mass exodus of the other single ladies out of the sitting room so they also excused themselves following the crowd behind Nicholas. The air was crackling with excitement, and all the ladies wanted to be part of it. The seven gentlemen still standing with their back to Light began to look over their shoulders as all the ladies left. They were confused as to what was taking place. Some of the ladies leaving were ones they were actively courting. Margo in particular was an heiress of considerable fortune with many admirers; two were part of the seven. Concern was creasing the brows of the gentlemen as they looked at the almost empty room. True to his word Nicholas approached where Light stood in the hallway by the grand staircase. Nicholas brought the entire female assembly along with him delighting them with tales of himself at the French court. The only persons remaining in the sitting room were the seven gentlemen, who now no one was paying any attention to and the elderly matrons, and all the gentlemen; many of whom now looked annoyed at the sevensensing that somehow they were at fault in chasing away all the beautiful women from the party. Nicholas quickly filled Light in on his role in the play they were about to perform. Luckily it was a play both men knew well, they'd often performed it for their grandfather as boys. Nicholas nimbly hopped midway up the grand staircase and waited until all the female's eyes were on him; he began reciting lines from the three musketeers. He threw himself into the performance and the ladies laughed at his antics and clutched their collective hearts in sorrow at the sad parts. Light did a passable Pathos he didn't have the flair for the dramatics that Nicholas did but because Samantha was in the crowd watching him, intently he rallied. He didn't want to either fail or fall short while her hazel eyes were on him. He threw himself into his role speaking to her only as he recited his heartfelt lines. By the time dinner was called three of the seven gentlemen had turned around to watch the performance. The remaining four, which included Rigsby, still had their backs turned to Light, but it was clear to everyone that they now felt foolish. The other gentlemen in the room had come out to join in as part of the crowd. They stood behind the ladies in support of the performance. 'If you can't beat 'em, join 'em' seemed to be their stand.

Chapter Thirty-Seven

Light paced well concealed in the old Butler's pantry ladder rehearsing what he would say to Samantha that night—her wedding was tomorrow. Here, he was sure no one would find him, and the servants had retired for the night. He heard the dull sounds of the pianoforte beautifully playing a midnight Sonata while the guests sipped Chardonnay and talked in low voices. He'd slipped away here to be alone with his thoughts. He planned to climb the trellis to Samantha's rooms on the top floor and speak to her shortly before midnight when he was sure she'd be alone. Her wedding to Rigsby was tomorrow morning at first light. But he still had a chance tonight to try to change her mind. He'd steal his chance if he could only find the right words. He had to convince her not to marry Rigsby. There wasn't a lot that he could say to her that she would believe. All of her doubts about him were true and what hurt most of all was that he had caused most of those doubts himself. If only he could go back in time to that cursed dungeon and redo their first encounter all over again. In his arrogance and self-righteous anger, he'd worked against himself that night. Now, because of those hefty mistakes, he might lose a chance to be with the only woman he'd ever really loved. He fetched his cousin's scotch bottle, and after ingesting some liquid courage he stood; his tall frame pacing anxiously as he rubbed his mother's wedding ring absently in his pocket. He wanted to give it to Samantha tonight, but instead of soothing him, the ring burned a hole in his pocket, reminding him of all he stood to lose. *Samantha,* he thought out loud mentally rehearsing his speech

"*I know why you've chosen Rigsby. I know that you're scared because of what Patricia told you.*" He practiced out loud.

Frustrated, he stopped in his tracks. W*hat the hell kind of speech was that? he sounded like an idiot.* He tried again, and the second attempt was even worse. This isn't going well, he muttered morosely to himself. Light marched over to the scarred wooden table and poured himself another small measure of scotch. Then another. He stretched his long legs and settled in pouring another.

*

An hour later his grandfather found him still sitting there staring somberly at the bottle. "I see that something is weighing heavily on your mind," the old man said knowingly, eyeing the half empty scotch bottle, Lady Liechfield's diamond wedding ring twinkling brightly next to it. Light looked up briefly, nodded and then went back to staring at his cousin's Scotch bottle as if it held all the answers he was seeking. MacDonald harrumphed "that bad huh" might have something to do with the fact that Samantha is getting married in the morning. Light did not respond; he simply looked up at the old man, scowled fiercely, and went back to staring at the scotch bottle. Thus, he was not prepared when MacDonald suddenly grabbed him roughly by the lapels and dragged him up to his feet. Stop moping about here like a little girl! he said roughly in a deep brogue. He continued yelling at his grandson, "Unless I've missed my guess you mostly got yourself into this mess and you're the only one that can get yourself out!" Stop hiding in here and go talk to her! Light shrugged off the rough grip and eyeing his grandfather skeptical he resumed his pacing from earlier. "Don't you think I know that!" he said roughly but the wedding is tomorrow, and there's nothing I can say now at this late date that can make her change her mind. Maybe if I had more time, he thought out loud. His grandfather made to reach for him again and Light agilely sideswiped him. He hadn't known the old man was still as strong as a bull and he was getting tired of being bodily manhandled. MacDonald was no light weight. He had reached for light with a rock hard grip, digging a frustrated finger into Light's shoulder as he spoke. The pain in Light's shoulder had bruised only his discipline had kept him from crying out. But now he was determined to avoid those beefy fingers. Light continued pacing. "Come on, lad, I taught you better than this."

MacDonald said, swiping a tired hand over his grizzled features. "I know you don't remember this but three years after you left our compound in the Highlands–I came looking for you. I hadn't heard neither hide nor leather from you since the day you left and I wanted to check on you myself and see how you were doing. I came into your big Sassenach house, where you were surrounded by a dozen tutors, etiquette instructors and scholars. They were busy helping you to unlearn everything I've ever taught you—they changed your speech pattern, they made you walk differently, they made you hold your head up high as if everyone and everything below your nose was beneath you. In short, they changed the man you were into the Duke, they needed you to be. You were the only male heir; without you the Dukedom would end. Believe me, they weren't fond of a Scott taking that lofty title but they had no choice, but first they had to strip you of everything that made you Scottish. That night, when you and I sat together over a meal, I could see that the Alexander that I knew was slowly fading away and becoming an old cold unapproachable soulless sassenach. My Alexander had been a man of laughter, caring, wise beyond his years, and very much connected to the land and his people. Many in our clan had even spoken of their intent to support your claim if you ever decided to be the next MacDonald. Alexander knows this—the real you are still in there somewhere. This week alone, I've seen more of the real Alexander than I have seen in a score of years. The more you're around Samantha the more the real you surface. I don't know why but the Alexander that I raised comes out more and more when you're with her. I know you must be having a tough battle inside of yourself, but for once, let the real you win. Go in there and speak to her from your heart. Whether you win or lose, you'll never regret that one Alexander. You'll never regret saying your piece. Light stared into his grandfather's eyes and the rest of the conversation continued between them with each other's eyes (without words). Then Alexander got up slowly gripped the old man's shoulders and brought him in for a deep hug. Light nodded to him, and wordlessly he left the Butler's ladder and instead of heading for the door, he exited through the window and one by one climbed the trellis up to Samantha's window.

Chapter Thirty-Eight

Samantha's startled hazel eyes flew anxiously to Light's face as he stepped agilely through her balcony window. He landed silently on the stone floor window entrance to her bed chamber. She had been staring so deeply and intently at the fire in her fireplace that she neither heard him climbing the trellis outside; nor heard him enter her window. She only turned when he was already inside as his feet touched the ground. For Light the moment her cool hazel eyes landed on him; he was at a loss for words; his carefully memorized speech evaporated as if it had never existed. Belatedly, he realized that she didn't exactly look like a happy bride-to-be. Rather she looked tired. Her eyes were strained and red rimmed as if she'd been crying but to him, she looked beautiful. "What are you doing here?" she said Horsley, her voice thin and threadbare. "You shouldn't be here," she said belatedly without heat or conviction. He didn't answer, he simply looked at her sad features and then opened his arms to her. She stared questioningly at him for some long minutes; his arms remained open. Then wordlessly she crossed the long distance between them, stepped into his arms and lowered her heavy head on his warm shoulder, sighing contentedly. He closed his arms possessively around her, breathing deeply of the lavender scents in her hair. How had this happened? How had she become so dear to him in such a short period of time and now just as he'd found her, he would be losing her forever as early as tomorrow morning. when she spoke her vows to another man. Unless…

(unless he could say something to her tonight to make her change her mind) he searched his mind for some words, but nothing came out. As her head was pillowed on his shoulder his lips touched the crown of her head then kissed down to her nose and finally dropped a kiss on to her lips. Perhaps his lips could do the talking for him; hers were ready and waiting, and they parted. I need he thought briefly penetrating her lips to sip on her tongue beneath, pulling her frame closer. Taking a deep steadying breath, he suddenly felt dizzy. *Samantha,* he thought silently to himself, *yes* her voice answered him quizzically. He was momentarily stunned he hadn't spoken the words out loud. They were connecting again through their mutual distress. That gave him hope that maybe it would be easier to find the right words if he didn't have to actually speak to them out loud. He pulled away from her lips; pulled away from her body it was too difficult to organize his thoughts when she was this close. Just the scent of her had him wanting to lay her down beside the fire and strip her clothes from her one by one. Samantha's startled hazel eyes looked up sharply at him and he decided to stop the trajectory of his thoughts. When they were this closely connected, he wasn't sure how much of his thoughts she could feel and judging by her startled look– it was quite a bit. He created some distance between them and resumed pacing. After some minutes he heard Samantha's voice as if from far away. "Was there something you wanted to talk to me about my Lord?" she asked, puzzled. He nodded but rather than speak he resumed pacing. Samantha went to go sit in a chair by the fire waiting patiently. "I think you know by now that I love you, and I can't say that I'm a man that is very well acquainted with love; actually, it caught me so by surprise that even after I thought I loved you, it took me some time to be able to put voice to the words or the emotions, he ran a frustrated hand through his hair." He wasn't doing this right, he was boxing this up, he could tell from the confused expression on her face. *Speak from the heart.* "I'm not sure what it is you're trying to say my lord, but I have to be up early in the morning," Samantha said. "Maybe we could have this discussion another time," she said quietly. Light became still. It was this moment. This was his moment and none other. He pulled out her grandmother's diary. On the day of your grandmother's wedding, she wrote this.

Oliver looked magnificent in his green wool suit. I can't believe the day is finally here. Today I'm finally going to be Oliver's wife. I have spent every waking moment in the last two weeks carefully knitting lace over the nightgown I will wear on our wedding night. I can't wait for him to see me in it. He always has a way of looking at me as if I'm the only woman in the world. On our wedding night, I want to feel like the only woman in the world for him because he is my world. No bride could be happier today than me

today...

He paused reading the diary and looked up straight at Samantha's eyes; her eyes had not let his face as he recited the well memorized words. "That's how every bride should feel on the day of her wedding. I suspect that you won't be feeling that way tomorrow morning when you stand next to Rigsby. And the question you should be asking yourself is why? And who would make you feel that way. I hope that it's me because you're my world, Samantha and if you would do me the honor of becoming my wife instead, I promise on all that I hold holy that you wouldn't ever regret it. I've made many mistakes," he said, closing the diary and putting it back inside the corner pocket on his jacket next to his heart; "but you haven't. Your instincts have been perfect. I ask you to trust in them one more time and choose me. I won't let you down. I love you. He pulled his mother's ring out of his pocket. Do me the honor of becoming my wife, he said earnestly, lowering his bulk on one knee." Tears streamed down Samatha's face as she stared open mouthed at his dear face. "She gave you her diary?" was her only response. How? Why? That must mean…

Samantha stared at Alexander for long moments, rising, moving closer, her arms going around him of their own volition. She memorized his features. "I can't." She breathed forlornly. "I've already given my word."

His massive chest momentarily seized and then recovered quickly he nodded jerkily, pressing his mother's wedding ring into her palm and wrapping her fingers around it in a tight fist. It belongs with you, he said giving her the ring, I won't be having any use for it. He stood and bowed deeply from the waist; he caressed her features briefly with his eyes and then like a cat he jumped nimbly out the large double barred balcony windows onto the trellis. In a thrice he was back on the ground floor his proud head held high as he walked away. He never took note of a pair of hazel eyes following his descent closely, bathed in a torrent of salty tears.

Chapter Thirty-Nine

Light woke up early on his beloved's wedding day. A big part of him wanted to be in London (as far away as possible from Evansdale and the church where she was getting married). Last night he'd considered fleeing post haste to his London Mansion to lick his wounds. But a darker more macabre side of him wanted to witness her nuptials. Or was it that he longed to see Samantha's face one last time. He wondered about himself for a thousandth time—*why would I put myself through this hell just for one last look at her. Am I that hopeless* Apparently so! He muttered as he got dressed. Simon walked into the dressing room with a pair of starched pressed dark wool merino trousers and a matching jacket. Light shook his head and pointed to his plaid kilt and matching plaid socks and jacket. Simon frowned in disapproval, taking a defiant stance. Light straightened his back and arched his brows in an immovable stance frowning in menace. Simon paused, studied his employer's body language, and grudgingly acquiesced. Their silent battle ended Simon humbly got down the Highland battle attire from its place of honor in the massive closet. As he dressed his Lord, Simon added a lot of English flair to the cravat's ensemble to ease his ire at losing this morning's battle of wits. All in all, Alexander looked imposing as he stepped out of Evansdale Manor heading to the church. He appeared every inch the Highland lord of good breeding that he was. He stood straight and tall as he marched to the small chapel and walked to the back row standing with his grandfather and Nicholas all of whom were also wearing the exact same Highland attire. The trio stood tall and proud in the back of the small church, a force to be reckoned with. Light's strong demeanor briefly cracked when Samantha appeared at the entrance of the church. His grandfather reached out and gripped Lights elbow in support. Light nodded his thanks imperceptibly. The family chapel was full, Grandmere, Bart and Serena sat in the front pew. Rigsby entered the small church prancing confidently he strode to the front of the pulpit, his arrogance and elation evident with every step. The guests stood waiting until Rigsby took his position next to Braying Ass, his best man. Samantha began walking toward Rigsby as the bagpipes played in the background. She was magnificent in a white wedding gown made of frothy white lace. The lace bodice clung deliciously to her curves then it swirled out wide at the hips; a long train floated around her feet like a cloud. In a white knuckle grip, she held a dozen purple violets. She also wore a thin transparent veil that covered her head. Her eyes, however, were strained and red rimmed as if she'd been crying but to Light, she'd never looked more beautiful. He drank in the sight of her while his jaw twitched. "Dearly, beloved," the harried parson began, "we are gathered together here in the sign of god and in the face of this company—to join together this man and this woman in holy matrimony," the parson droned on. "Marriage is commended to be honorable among all men and therefore is not by any to be entered into unadvisedly or lightly, but reverently, discreetly, advisedly, and solemnly. Into this holy estate these two persons present now come to be joined." Samantha looked up then, her eyes locking in with Light's; misery written on her face. *It's OK* he communicated silently to her easing her distress. She nodded upon hearing the unspoken words, her eyes tearing up more.

"If any person can show just cause why these two may not be joined together, let them speak now or forever hold their peace." A few heads turned in his direction even Samantha's grandmother turned and looked at him. Light rubbed his jaw in consternation. Oh, he wanted to object—very much so—but would Samantha forgive him if he did. He decided to keep his piece. His face grew warm under the tension of the moment, the parishioners questioning eyes in the church pews were still eyeing him. Gradually they turned around and returned their attention to the parson. The minister continue,: "Marriage is the union of husband and wife in heart, body and mind," on and on it went. At length Samantha looked up at Light again. "It is intended for their mutual joy and for the help and comfort given one to the other in prosperity and in adversity. Marriage is a lifelong consecration," ...on and on the parson droned.

"Are you well my love?" Light asked her silently in their clairvoyant way noting her apparent misery. She nodded.

"Why didn't you object?" She wondered.

He smiled at her question, shrugging. "I'm done being a bull in a China shop. Besides, I want you to be happy." he replied. She turned away facing her now malcontent future husband. Rigsby swiveled his head back and forth observing the silent dialogue between his future bride and Light, evidently annoyed that Samantha couldn't seem to stop looking at Light. His irritation evident.

"It is a moral commitment that requires and deserves daily attention." The parson labored on turning the page of his oversize bible. He lost his place and started over again. "Will you get on with it?" bellowed Rigsby at his wits end with the overlong sermon.

The small minister jumped, "I daresay this is most irregular, my lord—why I haven't even led the sacraments and said the lord's prayer. Why I haven't even..." He stopped mid-sentence as he watched Rigsby reach into his pockets. Rigsby smiled benevolently at the little minister and took out several guineas from his pocket, dropping them into the collection basket near his feet. The parson coughed discreetly and then turning several pages he rushed to the end.

"Do you Lord Randall Bradley III Marquis of Devonshire, take Samantha Rachel-Anne Minnis to be your wife? To live together after God's ordinance in the holy state of matrimony? Will you love her, comfort her, honor and keep her in sickness and in health, for richer and for poorer, for better, or for worse, in sadness and in joy, to cherish and continually bestow upon her your hearts deepest devotion, forsaking all others, keeping yourself only unto her for as long as you both shall live?"

"I will," stated Rigsby in a loud clear voice sliding his ring on Samantha's finger. The minister turned to Samantha hurriedly and asked her the same question.

She paused then shook her head in response. "Pardon me, miss," said the confused minister. "Shall I read it to you again?" he asked helpfully.

"Samantha," Rigsby said firmly, "answer the man. love—Lord knows I've aged a decade since stepping into this dank little place. Let's not drag this on any longer sweetheart. You're a beautiful bride. But please sweetheart, you know that I wanted to stand up with you at Westminster Abbey where all the nobles get married but to please you my beautiful bride I agreed to get married here at your Evansdale. But please dear heart let's not dally any further," he pleaded, smiling charmingly.

Samantha shook her head again, taking off his ring. "I can't marry you. I'm sorry but I would be making a grave mistake," she said. Fans began buzzing throughout the church like bees. Samantha ignored the shocked faces all around her. "I'm in love with someone else," she confessed heavily, seemingly relieved to have spoken the words out loud. On the front row Light saw Patricia stand up huffily and storm out of the church followed by an irate Rigsby.

Rigsby turned at the church door to hurl back one final insult. "To hell with this—and to hell with you, you Slag! If it's Light you're choosing over me, don't come crawling back to me when he's done with you, he changes women faster than he changes bedsheets." At hearing Samantha being insulted and called a Slag-Light vaulted out of his church pew leaping over three benches vitriol in his eyes. But Bart stood holding up his hand in a "stop right there" motion at Light.

Smiling broadly, he said, "This time allow me Light, besides he motioned with his head, I think you have a wedding to get to. Light looked longingly at Rigsby's departing back, his right fist itching to plant him a facer. But instead, he shrugged sheepishly and warmly clasped Bart's open hand. The two shook hands in harmony. Bart then left the church several loud thuds were clearly heard outside the church doors then silence. Bart walked back inside the church grinning broadly. He nodded once at Light and then sat down.

Chapter Forty

Her honor restored, Light loped over to Samantha and stopped halfway there. The strain of the last few minutes was taking its toll on her, and he didn't want to add to her distress. He would leave if she needed time to collect herself. He could wait. No one said a word. The assembly was glued to their seats as if watching a performance on Vaudeville. He saw the strain about her shoulders begin to loosen. He breathed a sigh of relief. He approached her as slowly as if she were a skittish mare, dropping down easily on one knee when he was still several steps away. He opened her grandmother's diary on the pink side and read an inscription in Latin in a clear baritone voice that carried across the church. He ended with confide in me semper, he added vine mihi numbered (*trust in me always—will you marry me*). Samantha could no longer see tears running down her cheeks, blurring her eyes. "I will," she said, nodding decisively, emotion making her shoulders shake. He closed his eyes saying a silent prayer of thanks. Then he rose gracefully and motioned for Nicholas to join him at the front of the church. Do you have a ring Nicholas asked worriedly, taking his place as best man, clasping his cousin warmly, and Moving Sir Thomas out of the way. Light shook his head. Samantha reached into her small lace sachet and pulled out Light's ring handing it to him. Light placed the ring in his pocket, smiling broadly, she'd kept his mother's ring. This day that ring had brought him much luck.

He then took out several large pound notes from his vest

pocket and handed a thick stack to the parson. "Oh, my sir – you're too generous," stuttered the stunned clergy, "did you want me to skip to the end?" he asked. Gratefully, tucking the notes under his voluminous robes. Light shook his dark head. Not at all drawled light. Take your time. I want to savor every minute. Go through all the sacraments, don't skip a thing. The minister smiled approvingly, opening his bible. He cleared his throat. Dearly beloved, the parson began we are gathered here. Oh, wait Samantha said impishly just one second father. I have just three little conditions for my soon to be husband. The minister looked at Light questioningly.

Light nodded for. "Go on," he said.

"It's about my family," she began hesitantly.

"Your family is always welcome to visit us in London anytime he said magnanimously."

"Oh no, not visit," she said sheepishly—live with us. I want my family to come live with us. Light coughed discreetly. Nicholas helpfully clapped him on the back.

"You look a little pale, Alexander, are you OK?" Nicholas inquired enjoying himself.

Light pinned his cousin with a silencing gaze. "Yes," he said to Samantha between coughs, "I would," (cough) "Love to have your grandmother and Bart live with us" (cough). He coughed again but managed to get the words out.

Samantha beamed at him and also, she continued, "I'd like to have my own pin money," she added, "to spend as I wish."

"Of course, my love." He nodded, adjusting his suddenly tight cravat.

"And lastly" she said sweetly, "I'd like that dungeon permanently destroyed." He grasped her hand warmly, turning to face her before the minister 'considered it gone." She nodded to

212

the minister for him to resume. He smiled at them both rubbing the large bank roll in his robes. Dearly beloved he bellowed animatedly. We are gathered here in the sign of God and in the face of this company—to join this man and this woman in holy matrimony.

Epilogue

Light was in his favorite place in his home. He was leaning back on his tufted leather back chair by a roaring fire in his library, a half empty glass of premium scotch whiskey sitting on a beveled table near him while his pregnant wife sat on his lap. He was currently halfway in succeeding to convince her to sneak upstairs with him. I'm not tired, she said, laughingly lightly at his antics. He nuzzled closer "it's not good for the baby if you don't get enough rest– he purred, I'll nap with you, he cajoled. God knows I'm tired, you wore me out last night. I think I got two hours of sleep the whole night, he lamented. And whose fault is that she teased in a throaty voice that was also musical. He never got tired of hearing that voice calling out his name in the throes of ecstasy. Their lips drifted toward each other as they always did when they were this close, his hand slid inside her bodice nuzzling her breast pulling her higher on his lap. "They're at it again" a disgusted small boy came out from his hiding place under his father's desk. Four-year-old Alex Lichfield pulled on his twin brother's arm pulling him out of their favorite hiding spot in the desk. Two identical hazel eyes peeing up at their parents, the twins were tall for their age, with light blonde hair and their fathers' stern features. Samatha beamed at her sons as they stood scowling at their parents. "Kissing again," scolded Alex, "yuck."

He scooted his mother away as he climbed onto his father's lap dragging his twin Nikolai with him. "Father, we drew plans of how to convert the rubble from the old dungeon into a real castle with a moat-see." He unrolled a long sheet of parchment onto the desk anchoring the ends with Light's signet ring and ink pot. His young face scrunched in concentration. "I found some drawings in this old book," he said, dragging up an engineering book that was bigger than himself.

"I'll let you gentlemen get on with your important planning," Samantha said sweetly, retreating. Light blocked her exit with his long legs but she agile side stepped him. Light watched her form as she walked away. Nikolai grabbed his father's chin, directing him to the large parchment.

"Look here, Dad," Nikolai said, "we can fill this area with water and make a real-life moat, the water can flow in from the lake. There's already drainage down there from some large pipes Alexander and I found them there last night."

Alex slapped his brother's arm in warning. "Um– I mean this morning– we found the pipes this morning," Nikolai amended.

Light looked sternly at his twin sons, "It's dangerous to roam the mansion at night- didn't I tell you both that already."

"Yes, sir," they said insincerely whispering quietly to themselves then smiling innocently at their father. Light looked from one pair of hazel eyes to the other tempted to be cross but finding it impossible. They worked their wiles on him as easily as their mother did. The drawing before him was quite good, it must be Nikolai's handy work. His brain was like a sponge. He remembered everything he read just like his mother. Alexander was the leader, always planning mischievous adventures; he was just like Light (his namesake). He adored his twin boys; he had as close a connection with them as he did with Samantha. He kept it a secret from them, but he read their thoughts as clearly as reading a book; that's how he always found them at hide and seek. All right he said enthusiastically if we're going to build a moat, let's do it big. He dipped his pen in his ink pot and added a drawbridge, a gate, brick walls and a keep. The three worked diligently for half an hour.

"Where are my monkeys," a gruff male voice called out.

"Uncle Bart is home yelled Alex lets go greet him," the boys raced off to greet their uncle headless of their father and the building plans. Light grabbed his scotch and followed his sons at a sedate pace. The boys were in the settee opening sweetmeats they wrestled from their uncle's pockets, searching energetically for more. A harassed Bigsby was attempting to pour tea to Samantha's grandmother and Caelin (Light's grandfather). The two elders had become close friends, wherever one was, you usually found the other. The only unhappy person in the house was Bigsby and Gordon Allen. Bigsby missed the dignified quiet of the old days. He failed to perform his duties with the same sonorous decorum that he'd managed before Light's marriage. It was mostly because of all the noise from the carefree boys who often used Bigsby as a tester for their pranks. Gordon Allen now the gardener missed the money and prestige of his former role. Lord light no longer needed his prior services. He'd closed his pleasure house and released each of his mistresses.

Light joined Bart on the settee sprawling his long legs in front of him sipping on his scotch watching his boys as they played. Bart had read for the bar three years ago and reopened his dad's original solicitor's office, which was doing far better now than it had under Walter. Bart and Serena were making plans to marry next month. Light was glad to have one less in law in his home, but he grudgingly accepted that he'd miss Bart. Bart had advised Light very well on a few key legal matters and besides being brothers by marriage they had a firm respect for each other and they both loved Samatha with a fierce loyalty.

You're my favorite uncle Nikolai said warmly giving Bart a bear hug. Bart ruffled his light blonde hair affectionately. "Hey!", said Nicholas throwing his hat to Bigsby and then throwing himself in an armchair. "I resent that. I'm your favorite uncle." The twins ran to Nicholas letting him swing them high in the air. You're not our uncle, you're our cousin, they squirmed under his arms as he carried them about like logs, hefting them on strong shoulders. Light smiled at all the mayhem in his home. He looked at his timepiece, Mrs. Lichfield should be stepping into her bath right about now, curling her toes happily in the warm water as she always did. He still had another hour before Bigsby served dinner. That should be enough time, he whistled a jaunty tune as he slipped out of the sitting room taking the stairs, two at a time.